FEARFUL FORTUNES AND TERRIBLE TAROT

WONKY INN BOOK 4

JEANNIE WYCHERLEY

Fearful Fortunes and Terrible Tarot
Wonky Inn Book 4
by
JEANNIE WYCHERLEY

Copyright © 2019 Jeannie Wycherley
Bark at the Moon Books
All rights reserved

Sign up for Jeannie's newsletter: http://eepurl.com/cN3Q6L

Fearful Fortunes and Terrible Tarot was edited by Anna Bloom @ The Indie Hub

Cover design by JC Clarke of The Graphics Shed.

Author's Note

This book, as with the whole of the Wonky Inn series, is set in East Devon in the UK.

It therefore uses British English spellings, idioms and vernacular.

*This book is dedicated to my wonderful friends and
dogparents*

Rob and Debbie Parker

With love, respect and sausages
Xxx

CONTENTS

CHAPTER ONE

"Is that a death threat?"

I crushed the letter in my hand as Charity rocked back on her heels in shock. "Seriously, Alf? Is that what I think it is? Let me have a look at it."

"It's nothing," I said, trying to laugh it off.

"How can you call it nothing?" Charity's forehead creased with annoyance as she reached for the ball of paper. Reluctantly I handed it over. It was my fault. I should have opened the envelope in the privacy of my bedroom. Here in the office nothing was sacred. My Wonky Inn Clean-up Crew were forever in and out and of course Charity had full access.

Not to mention Gwyn, my great grandmother, who was no respecter of boundaries.

Charity had snuck up behind me as I'd pored over the letter, rubbing my forehead in despair. She

1

glanced at it, then snatched the paper from me in shock. Moving a mug and a stack of papers from my cluttered desk, she smoothed the paper out, pressing down on it, as hard as she could, to iron out the creases. It was a plain white sheet of A4, with letters cut out to create a message.

"Somebody's been watching too many old-fashioned murder mystery movies," I quipped in a half-hearted attempt to ease the tension.

"It's not funny, Alf," Charity said quietly, examining the paper and not looking at me.

"Well you have to admit, someone has gone to absurd lengths to try and scare me. All that cutting out and sticking things down with glue. A print-out of a letter would have been anonymous enough. I mean, why bother?" I indicated our own printer and the pile of invoices in the tray. "Surely, these days no-one can tell the difference between one 'printer-that's-been-used-to-produce-a-death-threat' and any other?" I picked up the invoices, shuffled them neatly and then plonked them down on top of a leaning pile of admin on the corner of the desk. Charity caught them as they began to topple to the floor. She and I were like chalk and cheese. She liked to work in a clean and orderly environment, while I felt my creativity was hampered if I wasn't allowed to express myself through sheer confusion and untidiness. Somehow, between us, we muddled through

"My point is, it's not like the old days when the police could identify a culprit through the typewriter they'd used." I threw myself into my chair in exasperation.

"I can tell you're rattled," Charity said, drawing her lips together in a thin line.

"I am not." I studied my nails, in need of a file and a tidy-up. Black nail varnish covers a multitude of sins.

"You are so," Charity said, prodding me hard with a finger. I swear, at times she was capable of being the annoying younger sister I had been fortunate enough never to have.

"It's not the first letter I've received," I told her, and could have bitten my tongue off.

Charity rounded on me, her mouth a round O of astonishment. "Well how many have you had?"

I decided it was probably prudent to remain deliberately vague. "A few." Obtuse, she would have called it.

"Why haven't you told me before?"

I slumped back in my chair like some petulant teenager. "Presumably, because I didn't want to be grilled about them."

"I see." Charity sounded hurt. She dropped her head and I felt an instant pang of remorse.

In the ensuing silence I admired her hair, dyed bright green as an homage to the season of spring, which had been making itself felt and heard in the grounds outside Whittle Inn.

"Sorry," I apologised. "That was out of order. It's just that…I didn't want you to worry."

"Have you told George about them?"

"And I didn't want you to nag me to tell him either. George has enough on his plate without sorting out my little problems." She meant DS George Gilchrist, a local detective and my romantic interest.

"Is that how you see this? As a little 'problem'?" Charity smoothed the paper out again. Truth be told, I tried hard not to think of it at all.

I shrugged noncommittedly and Charity twisted her face up. Sighing in exasperation she read out the message, *"Time to leave, or time to die. Make your decision. Or we make it for you."*

We stared at each other, Charity's eyes wide, me grimacing slightly. "That's bleak, Alf. Horrible."

"Sticks and stones, Charity." I smiled, attempting to be cavalier about it all, but unsure whom I was trying to fool; her or myself. "Don't let it worry you." I reached for the message, but she snatched it out of my grasp. I'd have to wrestle her to get it back. I couldn't be bothered. I slipped down into my chair.

"Where are the other letters?"

"I binned them," I lied. "Which is what I want to do with this one. So give it back."

"Absolutely not. I think George needs to see this." Honestly, she could be such a mother hen. "Perhaps I should call Gwyn and ask her what she thinks?"

"No, no." I shook my head. "Don't get Gwyn involved." I'd never hear the end of it.

Charity placed the paper on the desk once more and glared at it. "The person sending this has to be local."

"Local? How do you figure that out?" I frowned. I couldn't see any clues as to whom it had come from or where. The postmark on the envelope simply said Exeter. That covered the vast area of East Devon and beyond.

Charity stabbed the page with her finger. "See these letters? Look at how they've been done."

Every letter – each about 2cm high, had been meticulously cut out and shaped to form itself. None of the words had been cut out whole, from a newspaper or a magazine, or other printed source. The overall effect was colourful.

"Very jazzy," I offered, and Charity gave me her best withering look.

"I recognize the colours and the style of the paper used to create this," she explained patiently. "I know exactly what has been used to form these letters."

I was impressed. "Go on."

"It's from a leaflet or a poster for an event that's happening in the village. I've seen it in the window of the café and on the noticeboard outside the post office. I don't think we've had any delivered up here so you may not have seen it yet."

"Why haven't we had any?" I asked. "Isn't Whittle Inn part of the community? I thought we'd got over all that anti-Whittle Inn feeling last October?"

"We did. I'm sure we did. The thing is, this poster is advertising an event that The Hay Loft is putting on."

"Ah." That made sense. The Hay Loft was my competition. There was an unhealthy rivalry between us, mainly on their landlord Lyle's part. He could be thoroughly unpleasant. I avoided him and his cronies as much as I possibly could. "So what's the event?"

"It's a Psychic and Holistic Fayre."

I narrowed my eyes. "What's that when it's at home?"

"You know...mind, body and soul...your sort of thing."

"My sort of thing?"

"Witchy. Fortune teller-y. Clairvoyant stuff..."

I shook my head in mock-shocked dismay. "I can't believe you just lumped me in with a load of amateur masseurs, hippie wannabes, and vegan-dream-catcher-manufacturers."

Charity guffawed. "Well *I* can't believe you didn't tell me about your death threats, so I guess that makes us even!" She cocked her head. "Are you saying everyone who attends these events is fibbing about their abilities?"

The sigh I emitted was deep and heartfelt. "No, I suppose not. It's just that so many of these folks aren't all they're cracked up to be at all. And what's more, they prey on the vulnerable. I hate that."

"How so?"

"Imagine you've been bereaved recently, and you badly miss that person. You desperately want to talk to the person you love again? So what do you do?

You contact a medium. The medium takes your money and offers you a few general platitudes that would fit anybody and everybody. Maybe they even say a few cryptic things that'll have you scratching your head. The so-called clairvoyant will give you just enough to make you believe what he or she is saying is true, but sometimes—quite often—it's more about them hoodwinking you. Many of these fakes have a good grounding in trickery, using psychology. They have a thorough understanding of human behaviour. They can read the '*tells*' we have."

"Like poker?"

I nodded. "Yes. Exactly! We give away a lot with our facial expressions and body language. When they watch us, they gauge how close to home they're hitting, and then emphasise the things we respond well to."

"Phew." Charity pulled a face. "Are any of them genuine? My mum loves this kind of thing. She's been to a woman in Durscombe for readings a few times."

"Oh of course, some of them are the genuine article. I don't want to suggest they aren't. But you must be on the lookout for fraudsters and opportunists. And I'm sure, if this Fayre is going to be as large as it is billed to be, then there will be plenty of those around."

Charity smiled. "Well given that you know so much about it, and you're the real deal, you really ought to go and offer your services."

"Pfft," I ejected in mock disgust. "Over my dead body."

Charity waved the death threat in my face. "Looks like somebody's already working on that for you."

I suppose I had been a bit slow on the uptake. Now that Charity mentioned it, I did remember the poster. It had been displayed on every available surface in the village for a week or more, and now as I strolled into Whittlecombe I noticed the giant A board on display outside The Hay Loft. This time instead of blithely ignoring it, I crossed the road and made a bee line towards it, intent on taking a closer look.

'The Largest Psychic and Holistic Convention in the South West!' the poster announced grandly in big bold letters. I resisted curling my lip and peered more closely at the smaller print.

'Come to a gathering of the world's brightest and

best fortune tellers, mediums, diviners, psychics and clairvoyants. Among our highly-sought after guests you'll find: Genuine Romany fortune tellers, Scandinavian rune-tellers, Pendle witches, African witch doctors, a voodoo priestess from New Orleans, and a Russian mystic.'

I sniffed.

It did sound intriguing.

I'd associated with a few talented Pendle witches whilst at school. Naturally gifted, they were still repressed by the traumatic history they seemed unable to escape. I'd be interested to meet them and perhaps make a few new useful connections. Maybe I could invite them to a retreat at the inn.

And a Russian mystic? That sounded most exotic.

Voodoo though? I whistled through my teeth. That was a little on the hard-core side for me. All that bloodletting and bone rattling. I preferred my fortune tellers to be of the gentle tea-leaf-reading variety. A little more British.

At the bottom of the poster, the blurb continued, *'Gifts stalls, food stalls, side shows, rides and displays. The tallest Big Wheel Devon has ever seen. Locally brewed cider and lemonade provided by The Hay Loft. Fun for all the family.'*

CHAPTER TWO

'When spring begins, you will meet your winter.'

I stared down at the new message. The colourful cut-out letters on the now familiar white paper mocked me. My hand trembled ever so slightly as my breath caught in my throat. The venom in these letters was escalating, and for some reason, this message stung more than any of the others.

When spring begins.

The first day of Spring in the northern hemisphere is also my birthday. March 20th. This year I would be 31 years old.

A sudden noise in the corridor outside my office startled me. I looked up to see Florence, my ghost of a head-housekeeper, gliding past the open door, dragging the vacuum cleaner along after herself. Florence wasn't fond of the vacuum, finding it overly heavy and cumbersome. She preferred a good old-fashioned carpet sweeper, or a straightforward broom coupled with a dustpan and brush. If she was carting around the heavier machine, it probably meant one of the guests had been particularly messy in one of the bedrooms.

I glanced down at the message in my hand again and shook my head. What should I make of these messages, and how much danger was I actually in?

Pulling open the bottom drawer of my desk, I rifled through a few items until I could put my fingers on an old leather folder at the bottom of the drawer. I tugged it free and flipped it open. There were over twenty messages—death threats if you like—that had been sent to me since I'd taken over the inn. The first few had been scrawled in untidy, angry handwriting, but from then on the letters had been cut out of coloured paper. The last three, as Charity had identified, had been snipped from the leaflets for the Psychic Fayre.

And yes, that suggested that whomever wished me harm lived locally.

Without examining the others, I filed the new threat on top of the pile, closed the folder and returned it to the drawer. Just in the nick of time. Charity bustled in as I re-organised staplers, hole

For all the wrong reasons, my gut told me, but I held my tongue.

The village, usually so peaceful, had become a hive of activity. Trucks and vans were queuing up to enter the fields behind The Hay Loft. As I stood and gaped at the activity, I could see flat-pack shacks and Portaloos being unloaded in the main field at the front, along with what looked like marquees. Different teams were working in different areas of the fields. To the right of the main field, the rides for the Funfair were being set up, including an enormous Big Wheel that threatened to dwarf the village, judging by the size of the components.

I stood by the gate, joining a small group of interested villagers including Mr Bramble, and my witchy best friend Millicent Ballicott. As usual Millicent was a sight to behold, sporting a neon yellow rain mackintosh, with purple trousers, bright red wellies—hand painted with yellow flowers and green ivy—and a rainbow coloured beanie hat. She had a tight hold of Jasper her hairy lurcher, and was clasping Sunny, the Yorkshire Terrier she'd adopted after the demise of Derek Pearce, to her chest. We all stood back, out of the way of the heavy vehicles. The field nearest The Hay Loft had to be where all the action would take place, with good access to the bar—handily for Lyle. The field at the back had obviously been requisitioned for camping.

I pulled my black Puffa jacket a little tighter around myself. Brrr. Camping in a field in Devon in March? No thanks. Next to a fun fair? That was a double no. You'd have to be hard-core.

Or crazy.

"It looks like it's going to be a big event," Mr Bramble said.

"Fun for everyone," Millicent sang, her voice merry with amusement. I caught her eye and she smirked, raising her eyebrows. She had the same thoughts as me then. She wouldn't be found dead in a tent, no doubt.

"Will you go along, Mr Bramble?" I asked. The old man had to be a likely barometer of what the locals would make of it all.

Mr Bramble shrugged non-committedly. "I'm not sure it's quite my bag, Alf, but Mrs Bramble is a different matter. She's always had a bit of a thing for Romany fortune tellers. Her Granny used to swear by them, apparently, and would never turn them away. I think it rubbed off on the rest of the family.

Yes, Mrs Bramble tells me she intends to cross some-one's palm with silver."

"As long as it's not the family silver you're parting with, Ernest," Millicent joked, and they laughed together.

"I'm sure she won't go that far, Millicent," Mr Bramble chuckled. He was a good-natured man.

I hoped Mr Bramble was right, I'd hate to see them lose the little they had to a prospective swindler.

"And ever since I was a lad I've loved riding the Big Wheel." We all gazed in awe at the size of the iron struts as they were hoisted into place by a huge industrial crane.

Whittlecombe had never seen the like.

Millicent's attention however, had wandered elsewhere. "Ooh look, Alf." She nudged me hard in the ribs. "There's the BBC camera crew." Sure enough, a large bearded man with a camera and a petite blonde woman with a large furry microphone were trailing along the path with a black-haired woman wrapped in an expensive-looking cream coat, teamed with green Wellington boots.

"That's Kylie Griffiths!" Mr Bramble uttered, his voice full of excitement and awe.

"You're a little old to be a fanboy, Ernest," Millicent tittered.

"I think she's lovely," Mr Bramble protested. "A voice like caramel."

"That's true," Millicent agreed. "Rich and deep. Quite unusual actually. Do you like her on the news, Alf?"

I had never seen the woman before. "I don't have a TV," I shrugged. That wasn't strictly true. There were a few television sets at the inn, but for the most part we only set them up when a guest specifically asked for one. From the moment I'd conceived the idea of the type of guest I needed to market for, I had understood that TV, Wi-Fi and the like, were probably not the reasons my guests would visit Whittle Inn. They came for the peace and tranquillity we offered, the beautiful setting and the non-judgmental company we kept.

Kylie smiled at us, then turned her back. "How's this?" she asked the cameraman.

He stared into the viewing screen and twitched his fingers to move her slightly sideways. "Yep. Good. Go for it."

Kylie nodded at the woman holding the microphone. "Okay. In three, two and one." She turned and addressed the camera, pulling herself tall and straight, speaking with an almost intimate tone to the green light.

"If you've ever wanted to know what the future holds for you, now's your chance. We've come to the small community of Whittlecombe today. It's similar to any of the dozens and dozens of villages you'll find scattered among the back lanes of East Devon, but for a week or so at least, there's going to be one important difference. The villagers are beginning preparations to host their first Psychic Fayre, and as you can see from the crowd gathering behind me, the locals are putting their all into this event and offering their full support."

Crowd? I wondered. There were six of us and two dogs. That hardly constituted a crowd in my book, although I suppose with a population of well under three hundred, six people by a gate on a week day wasn't bad going.

"Over the next few days, this modest field behind local hostelry, The Hay Loft, will be trans-formed into an extravaganza that may well encourage interest on a national level. Landlord Lyle Cavendish has joined me to tell us all about it."

She paused before addressing the camera opera-tive once more. "And cut. How was that?"

He nodded, and the green light turned to red.

I looked behind me. The normally scruffy and be-whiskered Lyle was loitering outside his pub, dressed in a suit. I'd never seen him looking quite so smart. He'd obviously had a shave and a recent hair-cut. Now he waited patiently for the camera crew to come and talk to him.

"Do we need to go again?" Kylie was asking.

The cameraman shook his head. "I just want to get some shots of the action in the field," he said. "Especially the construction of the Big Wheel. Give me five minutes."

"We'll go back to the van," Kylie nodded at him. "I could do with a warm through."

"It is a bit nippy today," Mr Bramble agreed, and Kylie turned to him and flashed a warm smile. Mr Bramble's cheeks tinged pink, and Millicent snorted in amusement.

"Are you looking forward to the Fayre?" Kylie asked the old man.

"Oh yes," he gushed, and I inwardly rolled my eyes. "I can't wait to see what's lined up for us."

Kylie nodded. "Perhaps you would say a few words to the camera for us, Mr ...?"

"Bramble. Ernest Bramble. Oh yes, I'd love to. Will I be on the news?"

I decided this was my cue to leave so I winked at

Millicent and pointed at an imaginary watch on my wrist. She waved me away.

As I turned to head back up the lane towards the little café where I expected to meet George, Lyle stepped in front of me and blocked my progress. I had to either stop and talk to him or move into the road. Another large truck ambled down the lane towards us, so I halted where I was and offered the landlord a thin-lipped smile.

"Alf," he said.

"Lyle."

"I see you're interested in the Fayre we're putting on."

"Seems to me as though the whole of the south west are interested in the fayre." I indicated Kylie, still chatting to Mr Bramble behind me. "It's of regional interest."

"If not national." Lyle smirked. "It's all good publicity."

"I wish you well with it," I said, trying to squeeze past him.

"That's very kind of you, that is." Lyle nodded thoughtfully. "Given that me and you are rivals and all that."

I smiled brightly; large and fake. "I don't

consider us rivals, Lyle. I think of us as competitors in an ever-expanding market."

"So you don't feel like we're stepping on your toes a bit then?"

I pondered on whom he meant by 'we'.

"Not at all. There's room for us both and I'm looking forward to coming and having a mooch around when the Fayre opens."

"Oh." Lyle exhaled, sounding regretful. "Oh, that's a shame that is."

"A shame?" I peered at him more closely. His tone said one thing, but his eyes shone in triumph. "What do you mean?"

"You're barred, Alf. We don't want you anywhere near the Fayre. Not the grounds, nor the inn. For the duration." He smiled down at me, his eyes reptilian. "Do I make myself clear?"

I gaped at him in disbelief. "Barred? What do you think I'm going to get up to?"

"You're a troublemaker," Lyle growled.

"*I'm* a troublemaker?" I couldn't believe what I was hearing. Lyle and his friend Gladstone Talbot-Lloyd had been instrumental in most of my problems when I'd arrived in Whittlecombe ten months before.

"You are. Everywhere you go, everything you do.

Look at the amount of trouble the village had when you invited that wedding party to your inn back in October."

"That was hardly my fault."

Lyle curled his lip. "Stay away, Alf. You're not wanted."

I shook my head, exasperated. "Fine."

Lyle nodded. "Good girl. I'm going to brief my security detail so that if they see you anywhere near here, they'll have carte blanche to take care of you."

I didn't like the way he said that. Or, the unhealthy gleam of hatred in his eyes.

"And that goes for your daft mate, Millicent, and that treacherous minx Charity too. You're all barred."

"Mr Cavendish?" Kylie's smooth voice called his attention. She was standing behind me. I wondered if she had heard any of what had passed between us. She gave no indication that she had. "We'd like to interview you in a minute, if we may?"

"Of course, of course!" Lyle was all hale and hearty, smiles and charm now. "Come inside where it's warm." I narrowed my eyes as he disappeared inside. "May I offer you some refreshments?" I heard him asking.

My fingers itched to cast a little spell to

make him choke on his drink of choice, but I remembered what my mother Jasmin had always taught me. What you send out into the universe you get back tenfold. Instead, I stilled my restless digits, took a deep breath and calmed myself.

There was no real need for me to feel slighted. I didn't want to go to his smelly old Fayre anyway.

"I have some bad news," George said.

The hand lifting my huge mug of hot chocolate topped with thick whipped cream, marshmallows and cocoa dusting, paused in mid-air, just short of my poised lips. I peered over the top of the mountain of cream. George certainly appeared troubled.

"Oh no." I frowned. "What's happened?" *Could this day get any worse?*

"I have to go away."

"Away? What? For a day? A weekend?" I returned my mug to its saucer and picked up my spoon. Maybe I'd try to eat the cream first. I stole a quick glance at George. He grimaced and shook his head.

"What do you mean? None of those?" My voice

sounded loud in the quiet café. Gloria glanced my way. "Not forever?"

"No, no, not forever, silly." George smiled. "I like that it sounds as though that would matter to you."

Was he fishing for compliments? "Of course it would matter to me." I modulated my volume.

He nodded, reassured. "I'll be away for a few weeks."

"Oh." I scooped a melting marshmallow and a blob of cream into my mouth. *Mmm. Heaven.* "Where are you going?"

"I can't tell you that."

"Oooh. Top secret!" I gushed, playing with him, but he didn't smile back. I lay my spoon back down.

"Not police business?" I asked, wondering why he was so reticent to talk about it. Did he have another woman somewhere?

I caught his fingers across the table and clutched his hand fiercely. He stared at me in surprise, and returned the pressure, probably imagining I was worried to be losing him, but instead I reached out with all my senses, listening to the rush of blood in his veins, and the beating of his heart, feeling his pulse and the way energy flowed throughout him.

I wanted to know he wasn't stringing me along.

After Jed I was taking no chances.

Satisfied, I released the pressure and entwined my fingers through his, stroking the top of his hand with my free hand. I could sense no artifice within him.

But he was troubled.

I twisted my nose up. "We can Skype," I suggested.

He shook his head. "No Skype."

"Phone me then." He shook his head again, glowering.

Where on Earth could he be going where there was no Skype? You could Skype from the moon these days, couldn't you? "It's okay," I said, disappointed but intent on trusting him.

"But it's your birthday. I wanted to treat you, and for us to do fun things."

My birthday. I thought of the letter, the death threat, hidden in the old folder in my desk drawer.

'When spring begins, you will meet your winter.'

George wouldn't be here on the first day of spring. I didn't need his protection, but I would miss his gentle support.

"It's okay," I repeated. "It's not a special birthday or anything."

"Every birthday is special." George squeezed my

hand. "And every day we're alive is important. We should celebrate at every opportunity."

I tipped my head to him, and pulled his hand across to my lips, kissing his fingers gently. "You're in a very reflective mood today," I ventured.

"I hate to let you down."

"Look, if what you're doing is important then that's good enough for me. We'll celebrate when you get back."

He nodded. "It's a deal."

"Lots of treats and lots of fun things," I reminded him.

"Lots."

I nodded. That would have to do.

I returned to the business of demolishing my luxury hot chocolate, aware of his eyes upon me. I glanced up, dabbing at the corner of my mouth with a napkin.

"I'll miss you," he said simply.

The soft expression on his face melted my heart. "I'll miss you too." I was suddenly aware how much I meant that.

CHAPTER THREE

E ven on a grey and rainy day in the middle of March, Celestial Street had a certain magic to it.

The brightly lit windows of the small shops glowed with bounteous warmth, illuminating the narrow cobble-stoned alley. The neatly ordered displays lured shoppers in with the excitement of brand-new goodies, deftly wrapped in brown paper and colourful ribbon by calmly magnanimous retail assistants. The enticing scent of freshly baked pies and cakes from the numerous bakeries called out to my taste buds, and my stomach rumbled. Four hours on a delayed train out of the west country to London and I felt hungry enough to chew my own arm off.

The Full Moon was my destination today. Wizard Shadowmender had sent a missive—by unknown and unseen courier—ostensibly requesting the pleasure of my company. In reality, it was less a request and more a demand. No-one turned an invitation from Luca Shadowmender down, not without good cause.

The public house buzzed with a mellow energy, fitting for the time of day. Staff were serving customers at the bar, and the tables were full of a rich tapestry of magickal folk gabbing over leisurely lunches.

I queued patiently at the bar, as always admiring the fixtures and fittings, scanning the optics and the sparkling glasses. The bar had long ago been decked out in oak. Some mighty mythical tree that had fallen in a great storm had provided the wood for the counters and the uprights, the shelving and the hooks. Now the old wood glowed in the certainty that it was well-loved, it had been tenderly polished to a deep, rich, golden reddy-brown by the passing of time; the gnarled edges worn smooth, the knots lovingly caressed.

I ordered a blackcurrant and soda water from a young and trendy witch behind the bar, so slim she would have disappeared had she stood sideways. She made me feel old, reminding me of myself, eleven years or so ago when I'd first started working in pubs in central London. Her face shone with the freshness of youth and the possibilities of life yet to come. She hadn't encountered The Mori, or anyone remotely like them. But then, to be fair, she wasn't fortunate enough to have a wonky inn keeping her grounded, either.

She indicated I should make my way through to the back. Wizard Shadowmender awaited me there.

I wound my way through chattering groups of witches and wizards, young and old and ancient. Some were cloaked, their robes dark and bland, their faces turned to the shadows. Others were brightly garbed, dressed in mundane clothes from the High Street. For my part, I dressed as always—in black from head to toe. No-one paid me any mind.

I found Wizard Shadowmender and my lawyer Penelope Quigwell occupying a booth in a small windowless room at the back of the pub. Lamps had been lit in here, and the fire burned, casting a cheerful light around the room, but Shadowmender and Quigwell had deliberately chosen a private spot where we would be neither overlooked nor overheard.

I slipped into the booth to join them and smiled my hellos to them both, curious as to why the old wizard had asked to see me.

"How are you, Alf?" Shadowmender asked.

"You look better than the last time I saw you. Not so fraught."

I laughed. "On the whole, things have settled down at the inn, now that we're up and running."

"I hear Whittle Inn is doing well." Shadow-mender nodded at Penelope to his left. I was struck again by how this woman was made up entirely of angles: tight black robes and a long billowing cloak covered a skeletal frame, sharp cheekbones and perfectly sculpted hair. Today she was wearing small square glasses with blue lenses, perched precariously on the end of her pointed nose. Her expression didn't change when Shadowmender alluded to her, but I saw her lips twitch and decided that was acqui-escence.

Perhaps she had shared my accounts with him. I sent her updates at the beginning of every month, which she passed on to an accountant. It helped us keep track of the finances of the estate. In return, she told me how much I could spend on the inn, or on the buildings in Whittlecombe, such as my cottages or Whittle Stores, all of which I had responsibility for.

I nodded, reflecting on the inn's performance. Interest in staying at the inn was growing slowly and bookings had been steady. I had collected several guests who'd already booked to return—several like Frau Kirsch for example—and there had been plenty of interest from ordinary mortal travellers over the summer season too. Word was getting around. Charity, Gwyn, Monsieur Emietter and my Wonky Inn Ghostly Clean-up Crew were proving their worth over and over.

"Better than I might have hoped," I answered thoughtfully. "And now I'm making inroads into the work that needs doing in the village."

"Progress is steady," Penelope confirmed.

She was a cold fish, but she certainly kept me in line. After a rocky start, I'd grown to appreciate her, although I had never really warmed to her.

"That's good news," Shadowmender approved, then indicated the menu. "I've taken the liberty of ordering lunch, Alf. I hope you don't mind?"

At that moment a waitress appeared with three steaming plates of food. She deftly placed one in front of each of us. A thin broth for Penelope, a Ploughman's lunch for Wizard Shadowmender with a huge chunk of cheddar cheese and a large bowl of ploughman's relish, and a steak and kidney pie with cabbage, mash and gravy for me. My mouth drooled. I glanced up at Shadowmender and his eyes twinkled at me. The lovable old rogue had known exactly what I would have ordered given the opportunity.

I tucked in. "Sorry I was late," I said between mouthfuls. "The train was delayed."

"I heard you passed your driving test?" Shadowmender replied.

"Yes, I did. Not that I'd drive all the way up here." You'd have to be bonkers to risk the South Circular around London. "No, I'll let the train take the strain, as they used to say."

"Very sensible." Shadowmender broke off a chunk of bread and chewed hard. "Any more sighting of our friends?"

I knew exactly whom he meant by 'our friends'. I shook my head. "No. All quiet on that front for a while, although in some ways that always makes me a little uneasy."

"The last time you saw them was in your tenant's bedroom?"

"No." I shook my head, swallowing a piece of my deliciously rich pie. "I mean, yes, I did see them then, but I saw them again the night of the wedding we hosted at Halloween. There was one in the hedge. I thought it was fairy lights at first, but it definitely wasn't."

"A big one?" Shadowmender asked, casting a

quick glance around at people moving about in our general vicinity. I watched them too, equally filled with suspicion. You could never be too careful. The Mori were devious after all.

I dropped my voice. "No. It wasn't any bigger than a cricket ball. Much smaller than ones I saw before."

"And the one in the bedroom?"

"About the same size."

Shadowmender nodded. "They could be probes, sent out to keep an eye on things."

That made sense, mostly. "But Derek, my tenant?"

"You said he'd been dead for some time."

George had passed those details onto me from the pathologist's report. "Yes, potentially twenty-four hours or so."

"It may be that Derek was killed by one of our friends," Wizard Shadowmender said, "and one of the probes lay in wait, watching to see who would turn up."

"Presumably they didn't know it would be me." I swirled my forkful of mash into the gravy, trying hard not to think too much about Derek lying on the floor where I'd found him, with one hand stretched out, and his terrified Yorkshire Terrier making a bolt for the door downstairs.

"No." Shadowmender sat back, his bread and cheese forgotten. "Which has to make us wonder who else they thought might visit Derek."

That wasn't something I'd considered. Now I thought about it, I could see that the orb hadn't tried to attack me. It had just frightened me off, and then smashed its way out of the window. If it had been waiting for someone else, would it have delivered a message, or would it have killed that second person too?

We finished eating in silence, minds whirring with unspoken thoughts, until the waitress broke the spell by coming to collect our plates. "Would you like dessert?" she asked. "The cheesecake is on special."

How could I resist?

Coffee along with Wizard's Cheesecake followed shortly. Chocolate biscuit base, white chocolate cheese mixture, blueberry compote that turned everything an alluring bluey-purple and a sprinkling of hundreds and thousands, all topped off with a fizzy sparkler.

"Happy birthday, Alf," Shadowmender said and tucked into his own piece. Penelope looked on as we munched, certainly austere about the number of calories she put into her tiny frame.

When we'd finished, Shadowmender sunk back into his chair and rubbed his belly. "Too much," he moaned, and I had to agree.

I leaned forwards across the table. "Why did you ask me to meet you up here in London? It can't have been just for an update about my sightings of spinning globes."

Shadowmender's eyes darkened and he nodded, casting a quick glance at Penelope. He motioned for the waitress to clear away the plates, and we sat in silence as she wiped the table down before leaving us alone once more.

Wizard Shadowmender leaned in closer, and Penelope joined the huddle. In a quiet voice the old wizard confided in me. "I need you to undertake a little mission for me, Alf. I considered asking Mr Kephisto, but I fear he is too old. I need someone a little younger with a dash more energy." This seemed slightly unfair on Mr Kephisto. I wasn't entirely sure how old he was, but he was as fit as a fiddle and extremely energetic for his age.

"Penelope has managed to unearth some information that has us both worried." He looked me directly in the eye. "What I'm going to ask you to do could be dangerous." He held one hand up before I could interrupt. "It may not be and there might be nothing for you to worry about, but I can't be sure. Nobody can. You will need to be on your guard."

I nodded silently, many questions forming on the tip of my tongue, but I knew Shadowmender would tell me everything I needed to know. "Alright," I said.

"You recall you sent us images of some documents you found in Derek Pearce's cottage?"

Of course. I'd found a folder in the corner of a drawer in his deceased son's bedroom. Bank statements, with one large and recent deposit.

"The deposit had been sent from a company called Astutus?" Shadowmender's voice was so quiet I had to strain to hear him. He looked over at Penelope and she took the thread from him.

"I've had a few people looking into that company and it's been very hard to track them down. On the one hand they're a company in the public domain, but when you look more closely they are simply a façade, a shop front for something or someone else." Penelope frowned. "I have some of the best researchers in the business. A few technical wizards with amazing financial acumen, and a number of business witches who can unlock anything with the right combination of spells and positive intent."

Penelope's eyes flicked towards a movement in the booth behind me and we all waited. I held my breath, my fingers twitching nervily in my lap.

When the people behind us left and the waitress finished clearing up after them, Penelope leaned in once more, so close I could feel the warmth of her breath on my cheek. "We finally though we were making some progress, that we'd found some accounts relating to Astutus, when suddenly every one of our machines downloaded a nasty virus and we were forced to abandon all tracking. By the time we managed to get our systems up and running again, Astutus and all traces of them had disappeared."

I nodded, a sharp pang of fear poking my innards. We were dealing with something seriously dark here.

"All except for the records we had managed to download. This turned out to be the most recent bank statement from an account held in a bank in Switzerland. We're looking into all the transactions listed on that statement – and unfortunately for us the statement was incomplete - but one that you should definitely know about for now, is for £10,000 paid on the first of the month to one Lyle Cavendish."

My mouth dropped open. "The landlord of The Hay Loft in Whittlecombe?" I gasped in quiet shock. There was the evidence, if we had ever needed it, that Lyle was directly involved in something decidedly dodgy.

Penelope noted my expression and held a pale thin hand up quickly. "There are two things we can infer from what we've found, although we have to be careful that we don't jump to conclusions without further evidence." She flicked a beautifully manicured finger up in front of my nose, her nails painted blood red. "Firstly, Lyle Cavendish has received a payment from the same company that deposited money in Derek Pearce's account. There may or may not be a connection between Astutus and...our friends... but it seems to be too convenient to be a coincidence."

I agreed. "And the second thing?"

Penelope flicked a second finger up. "This wasn't a one-off payment. The record clearly shows this was a direct debit. Cavendish receives the same payment on the first of every month."

Gob-smacked I sank back into my seat. "Wow. That's a lot of money."

Shadowmender looked from Penelope to me and

then back again. "We do need to be careful what we surmise of course, but yes, you're right."

"We don't know how long the direct debit has been set up for. It may well be that this was only the first or the second time this amount of money was deposited in Lyle's account, but it's plain that the *intention* is for the payment to be more than a one off." Penelope sat back, satisfied she'd completed her task of filling in my knowledge.

What did Lyle do to warrant that amount of money from The Mori, if indeed Astutus were my adversary? No wonder his inn made it through the winter without scrimping and saving. Lyle was having no problem paying his bills. It looked like they were all being covered for him.

And the cost of the Fayre? No doubt that was being paid for too.

"He's just about to host the largest Psychic and Holistic Convention the region has ever seen," I said. "I couldn't understand how he was affording it, but now I think I know."

This obviously hadn't passed Wizard Shadowmender by. "And that brings me to what I'm going to ask you to do, Alf," he said, his face deadly serious. "You can say no of course."

I'd momentarily forgotten that the old wizard

had a task for me. I shook my head. There was no way I'd say no when the future of my wonky inn depended on keeping it safe from The Mori. I'd do anything to ensure the safety of Whittle Inn and the ghosts who inhabited it.

"It's a multi-pronged mission that I'm hoping you'll be able to help us with. Penelope needs more information about Astutus, so that's the first thing we need you to keep a look out for. It certainly feels as though there's a hive of activity and the locus appears to be in or around Whittlecombe."

Ears and eyes to the ground then, I thought. That seemed simple enough, although I wasn't sure how much I was likely to find out given The Mori's over-reaching commitment to secrecy.

"Secondly, we've had some secret intel about this Fayre of Lyle's. I need you to get in there, amongst the traders and attendees, and find out more for us."

Now that was going to be impossible. "I can't do that," I said, dismayed. "Lyle's banned me."

Shadowmender glanced at Penelope and then back at me before roaring with genuine merriment. I spotted Penelope's lips turn up in the ghost of a smile.

"You give up too easily, Alf. Never say never!"

CHAPTER FOUR

Never say never indeed.

One week later, with the Fayre about to open, I found myself concealed in a caravan on the back field behind The Hay Loft, peering out of thick lace curtains at the other inhabitants of the field as they came and went, getting ready for the grand opening.

Or rather my alter ego scrutinised the competition, for I had agreed to a magickal makeover for the purposes of Shadowmender's mission, and the caravan wasn't just any caravan. Far from it. The centre for Undercover-Operation-Psychic-Fayre, was no less than a genuine Romany caravan. This horse drawn construction, well over a hundred years old, had been beautifully kitted out in glorious bohemian grandeur.

When I'd initially taken delivery of the caravan

and Neptune, the enormous carthorse that came with it, (at a services off the A30, with a B road access I could drive the horse down) I'd spent an excitable thirty minutes simply opening and closing all the little cupboard doors and drawers, peering behind privacy curtains and examining the neat accessories and equipment the caravan had been kitted out with. There was two of everything I could possibly need – glasses, mugs, bowls, plates, knives, forks, spoons, a frying pan and a couple of saucepans, a small larder stocked with provisions, and colourful quilts, pillows and cushions and so on. I loved the sheer eclectic nature of the ensemble. Nothing matched, and yet thanks to the explosion of colour, everything worked together beautifully.

Neptune and I had clip-clopped down the lane to Whittlecombe, gaily holding up the traffic. I'd waved cheekily at any motorist who glanced my way, and once I'd arrived at the field behind The Hay Loft, I discovered that Wizard Shadowmender had arranged for Neptune to stay at a local stable. He'd thought of everything.

Such fun! I couldn't begin to imagine where Shadowmender had sourced the caravan. He obviously had some amazingly trusting friends. To my mind, inhabiting it was a little like being on holiday.

Or it would have been if there wasn't serious business to attend to.

I'd had to tell Charity I'd been unexpectedly called away on urgent family business to London. I hated lying to her, but for the time being, I really had little choice. I'd also sought out Gwyn to spin her the same story, but Grandmama being Grandmama, didn't believe me for a moment.

"You can't lie to me, Alfhild. I can see right through you," she'd scolded, and I recognised that as a truth on several levels. She and I were much alike, and she could tell when I wasn't being straight with her.

"Grandmama," I'd whispered frantically, "I don't mean to be evasive but right now I can't tell you what's going on. As soon as I can share, I will. I promise." She stared at me through wise eyes, scrutinising my face. Eventually she'd nodded.

"Very well."

"I need you to work with Charity and make sure the inn remains secure without me. Keep it ticking over and if there are any issues...," I meant with The Mori or their like, "...then insist that Charity calls Millicent straight away. It's vitally important—as you know—that the protective circle stays in place around the whole of the grounds."

"Of course, my dear. You know we will do everything necessary." Gwyn had been a magnificent witch in her day, so I'd been told, but I'd never seen a ghost perform magic. Nor had she ever attempted to, or acknowledged she could, in my presence. I trusted her with the running of the inn and she'd be a huge help to Charity, but I needed Millicent to be available for emergencies.

"And you're welcome to use my bed," I said, sniggering quietly, knowing exactly what was coming.

"*My* bed," Gwyn retorted. "The one that *you're* borrowing from *me* until you end up spirit side."

"Yes, Grandmama," I laughed. "Whatever you say. You will look after Mr Hoo for me too?"

"Don't worry about a thing." Gwyn tutted. "Honestly, you must think Charity and I are amateurs."

I smiled. "Love you, Grandmama," I'd said and skipped out of the inn, certain in the knowledge there was nothing that Gwyn and Charity couldn't handle together.

My transformation had taken place in a small rundown house in Bristol not far from the IKEA superstore there. Rather than head all the way back to Celestine Street and London, Shadowmender had organised for a Cosmetic Alchemist to meet me at a safe house in the city—about halfway from home.

From the busy road, I'd climbed the steep steps to the three-storey terraced building's dusty door and tapped tentatively, my knees knocking thanks to having no clue what was about to happen to me. A rotund lady, middle-aged, with bleached blonde Marilyn Monroe type curls and three-inch-long nails answered the door relatively quickly. She showed me into the front room, chewing all the time on a wad of gum. A battered sofa and an old-fashioned TV with heavy buttons, a stained 1970s coffee table and a worn armchair did not inspire me with confidence. The whole house stank of cheap school dinners, and a faintly unpleasant and acrid musky scent that I didn't much like.

What on earth was the house used for under normal circumstances? It didn't bear thinking about.

"I'm Alfhild Daemonne," I told the woman. She looked me up and down from head to toe then back to my head and down to my toes once more.

"Interesting," she said, chewing on her gum.

My left eyebrow twitched nervily as I awaited her verdict, my teeth clenching painfully together.

"Wizard Shadowmender wants you to have a complete makeover," she said, and looked carefully at my face. "That's a bit of a shame because you do have the most beautiful hair."

"Thank you," I said. *I think. What about the rest of me?*

"Are you okay with that?" she asked, popping her gum quickly.

I gulped. "I guess so."

"Oh I wouldn't worry about it too much." The woman softened and smiled. "You know it's only temporary, right? I can give you a spell—like a bath bomb—you add it to your bath, and it will transform you right back almost instantaneously."

"Oh." I sighed with relief. "That sounds great."

"Good, good." The woman appraised me once more, then held her hand out. "You look a little nervous, Alfhild. I'm Cordelia Denby, by the way."

I relaxed a little. "Call me Alf."

"Rightio, Alf." She gestured at the door. "What we're going to do is head on upstairs where I have a special room. You'll take you clothes off in the waiting area, put on the robe that's provided there and then when you're ready just slip through to the treatment room. Let's go." I followed the woman out of the dank and dismal living room and climbed the carpet-less stairs to the next floor, our footsteps echoing around the largely empty house.

"Here we are." Cordelia held the door to the changing room open. It was clean, at least. Little more than a cupboard, it had been freshly painted, and a stool had been provided to perch on. A second door opened into the next room. A long white robe awaited me on a hook, and there was additional space for me to hang my own clothes. "When you're ready just come through that door. It will be dark. Take two steps in and close the door behind you and after that I'll guide you through the rest of it."

She disappeared, and I closed the door after her. I quickly undressed and slipped into the robe, tightening the cord around my middle. Taking a deep breath, I opened the second door. As I did so, the light in the changing room flickered off behind me and I was plunged into darkness as Cordelia had promised. I took two steps in and waited. The door closed, and I felt a hand reach out to take my arm.

"I'm just going to slip you inside this tent. Can you feel the material in front of your face?" I reached out and my hands made contact with something silky. "That's it, just take another step forward, and yes, you're in. Good."

The material was arranged behind me.

"Now, just take the robe off for me, lovey." Grimacing, I unknotted the robe and slipped it off. Cordelia must have reached for it because a second later it had been tugged free of my grasp. I heard a zipping noise as I was enshrouded by the tent.

Thankful for the dark to spare my blushes, I waited patiently, listening to Cordelia moving around the room. I recognised the sound of chair legs scraping against a wooden floor, then a whirr and a click, and a couple of red lights appeared on a console in the corner, illuminating the room ever so slightly. As I'd thought, I was standing in the centre of a tall circular tent, little more than a silk transparent curtain really. Numerous machines surrounded me. Cordelia was sitting in a state-of-the-art leather chair, like something you might use if you were playing an all-immersive computer game. She sported a pair of thick goggles and had a keyboard to her right.

"What are you planning on turning me into?" I asked, my voice quaking along with my knees.

"Oh, Alf," Cordelia grinned, obviously relishing this aspect of her job. "You're all set to become Fabulous Fenella the Far-Sighted. Just turn slightly to your right, my love. Chin up. Great stuff." She tapped a couple of buttons on the keyboard, and I heard a couple of the machines whirl into life. The tent rippled around me, trembling in a sudden violent breeze.

"Yeeha!" Cordelia sounded for all the world like some strange demented cow-girl. Her chair twisted and rolled as she thumped keys on her keyboard, making the lights on the console dance. "Let's do this!"

Fabulous Fenella the Far-Sighted had her own decorated booth at the Psychic Fayre to match her luxurious and quirky caravan. She—or rather I—stood outside the booth admiring the newly painted sign that spoke of my skills as a fortune teller, using none other than Shadowmender's Christmas present to me. He'd insisted I utilise his scrying orb as a crystal ball.

I'd swapped my usual black ensemble—long black skirt and jacket over a black t-shirt, accompanied by wild red hair—for a calf-length midnight blue dress that buttoned through the front, with matching slip on shoes. This in turn corresponded with my blue-black sleek bobbed hair and deep blue eyes. I'd been aged, but only to about forty or so. I wore my hair twisted in a headscarf, and large silver hoop earrings. My lips were thinner, and my cheekbones more pronounced. In fact all of me was more pronounced because I was slimmer than I'd ever been as an adult. I quite liked that aspect of it, but memories of super-slender Penelope Quigwell supping at her mean beef broth reminded me of the sacrifices I'd have to make in order to remain slim.

And given that immediately to the left of my booth, there was a young woman selling freshly baked brownies of every flavour imaginable, I wasn't entirely up to the challenge of remaining penuriously slim.

To the right of me, a small A-board announced Kooky Kahlila was 'in residence' in her booth. It turned out that the middle-aged woman currently hovering next to the entrance, nibbling on a melted caramel brownie and wearing jeans and a fleece jacket was none other than Kahlila herself. She spotted me reading her sign and skipped over to say hello.

"You must be Fabulous Fenella the Far-Sighted," she said, holding out her hand, spiky black nails armed and ready.

"The very same." I smiled, feeling like the biggest fake possible, but curious about her casual

FEARFUL FORTUNES AND TERRIBLE TAROT

attire. "And you're Kooky Kahlila?" I nodded at her sign.

"Yeah, well, kind of." She giggled. She had a strong Essex accent, reminiscent of a few people I had known in London who hailed from Canvey Island. She hung on to each word for dear life, clearly pronouncing each—lazy on the first syllable, emphasising the last, and creating plurals when there really didn't need to be any. I found her instantly charming and likeable.

"My real name is Carole Jones. Can yous believe that? There is nuffink mysterious about the name Carole. Am I right? So I 'ad to become Kahlila. It sounds right exotic, don't it?"

I laughed, genuinely amused—her warmth seemed infectious. "Yes it does."

"And what about you, Fabulous Fenella? Are you mysterious as well as fabulous?"

"Oh I'm both those things," I said and winked. I was pleased my voice at least still sounded like me even if I looked nothing like myself.

"You're a crystal ball gazer?" Carole asked, examining my colourful sign with interest.

"Yes. When it wants to show me things." I'd been secretly hoping that no-one would pay any attention to my sign, or trouble themselves to visit my booth.

That way I wouldn't have to try to be fabulous or mysterious. I'd only ever used the scrying orb at Christmas when I'd been attempting to track down Mara the Stormbringer. But needs must. I was undercover. Wizard Shadowmender had assured me that I knew enough magick to be able to coax the orb into action.

That remained to be seen.

"What about you, Kahlila?"

"A bit of this and a bit of that, you know how it goes. I do a bit of spiritual healing."

"What's that exactly?" I asked, curious as to the form spiritual healing would take.

"I can make a person well by using a spirit guide. You know some folks, they don't really like taking pharmaceuticals, so mine is an approach that can work for them."

"You're a shaman?"

"That's right, Fenella. I am." She moved her hands through the air outlining her head, crossing over her heart and then dropping them gracefully towards the ground. "I allow a spirit to enter me, to flow through me and then I channel that energy in such a way that I can empower others." It was a neat movement, vaguely yogic. Very new-age.

I'd heard about such complementary therapies in

the past, but I'd never come across a real shaman before, so this was quite exciting.

"Wow, I'd love to know more about that," I enthused. I loved the idea of working with spirits to bring about health and wellness. I wondered whether I could channel any of my ghosts to rejuvenate another person. Then I thought of Gwyn's stern face and decided it probably wouldn't work. She would scare the poor patient to death.

"Well we should get together over coffee and maybe swap a session or two. After all, we're here all week, ain't we?" Carole laughed gleefully.

"We are that," I said.

I spotted Lyle in my periphery vision and shrieked inwardly, forgetting that he wouldn't recognise me in my current state. "Can you just excuse me for a minute, Kahlila? I need to head back to my caravan to grab a few things."

I didn't wait for her response, just hot-footed it through the damp grass, returning to the camping field as fast as my new-to-me little legs would carry me.

An hour or so later, after fortifying myself with a

strong cup of tea and half a packet of chocolate hobnobs, I ventured out of my hidey-hole in search of some other new faces.

The Fayre had yet to officially open but there were quite a few people milling around already. For the main part they were store holders and suppliers. There were several smaller vans dropping off supplies to the stalls that needed provisions, and at the entrance and rear of the main field there were several large catering vans setting out their own spaces.

There was the usual food on offer. Good British fare: fish and chips of course, pies, seafood—along with several US style vans, offering burgers and pizza. There was a small hot dog stand, with a candyfloss booth next door to it, spinning wisps of pink sugary sweetness into gossamer fairy wings. None of these seemed particularly healthy or holistic to me and spoke volumes about Lyle and the culinary choices presented at The Hay Loft.

However, there were plenty of healthier food treats on offer too. Several vegan stalls, including one that specialised in Middle Eastern food that looked particularly scrumptious, and an Indian food stall serving curries, pakoras and roti.

But my eye was drawn to a liveried van that

looked like something straight from the 1930s. The hatches had yet to be pulled open, so I could clearly read the lettering. Outlined with a lush gold flourish were emblazoned the words, "Robert Parker Esq., Whittlecombe. Purveyor of Perfect Pork Products."

A local trader selling sausages. How magnificent.

I added him to my list of must-eats and turned about to resume exploring.

But as I about-faced, I walked smack bang into one of the tallest and widest men I'd ever seen. In fact, he was so large, he'd probably hardly noticed I was there—especially given my newly diminutive Fenella state of being.

I'm certain he'd have noticed me as Alf.

"I do beg your pardon," I exclaimed to the walking man mountain. I had a mouthful of sheepskin jacket and struggled to see above the felted fronds that hung from the neck and arms. He took a step back and stared down at me, all long floppy salt-and-pepper hair and magnificent beard. If ever a man looked like a Viking close-up, this was it.

"No, no," he said. He had thick accented English, so I rapidly made the assumption he was indeed Scandinavian or something close. "Please. My fault. I wasn't looking where I was going." To be fair, he probably was looking in the direction he was heading, but not actually looking down at the ground, inhabited by us mere earthlings. He blinked down at me and I became aware of what I must look like, staring up at him, my head tilted back, open-mouthed, catching flies and not saying anything sensible.

"I'm Alf, no I'm Fenella," I said, kicking myself, and shot my hand out to shake his. He offered me an enormous paw that could have swallowed both of mine in one fist.

"Morton Arnesen," he smiled, his moustache and beard twitching in amusement, at my display of ineptitude no doubt. A man in his late fifties, his hair had probably been blonde once upon a time and had now turned to a grizzled white. He had a warm complexion, glowing with ruddy good health, the face of someone who spends a lot of time outdoors.

"Where are you from?" I asked, hoping to recover some poise.

"A pretty little place called Bremanger."

That meant nothing to me, and I stared up at him through wide eyes, waiting for him to tell me more. He obliged. "Bremanger is a village in Bremanger Municipality in Sogn og Fjordane county. In Norway," he added when I rewarded his explanation by continuing to look clueless. "I live on the Bremangerpollen bay on the western side of the Bremangerlandet island."

"Is that close to anywhere..." I paused, bashful about displaying my ignorance. What I meant to ask was '*is that close to anywhere I might actually have heard of?*' but I didn't want to come across as some sort of Anglo-centric doofus.

"Not really," Morton shrugged. "It's pretty remote." Then he winked at me. "It's far north of Bergen."

"Ohhh," I drew out, relieved to hear a word I recognised, although to be fair, I'd have better luck pinning the tail on a donkey blindfolded, than finding Bergen on a map of Norway if it wasn't in huge letters and highlighted in neon orange.

"You're a long way from home. Are you here for the Fayre?" I asked quickly, intent on covering my ignorance by moving to safer ground.

"Yes, I read runes. Well actually I cast stones, but these days it is better to say you read runes as that seems to have more meaning to potential customers." He smiled, a huge jovial grin that illuminated the grey day. "And what about you, Alf ... Fen ... Fen..." he tripped over my name.

"Fenella. I read a crystal ball." At least I hoped I did.

"Ah fascinating. We shall have to swap a reading each." He pointed to the camping field. "You can find me in the big family tent in the corner of the field. You can't miss it as I'm flying the flag of Norway. Or, just pop into my tent here on the field. It's the big one made of reindeer skin."

Poor reindeers. "Great," I replied. "Nice to have met you, Morton. We'll catch up soon."

I watched him stalk away, great strides for an enormous man. He covered the ground twice as fast as I could have.

I turned back to the sausage van. Still closed. I was intrigued as to whom among the locals of Whittlecombe might own it. However with no sign of life, it looked like I'd be scrounging my dinner from elsewhere. I continued my tour of the field as a light drizzle began to fall, which succeeded in making the grass slightly slippery underfoot, soaking through my ridiculously impracticable shoes. I determined that from now on it might be better to wear my wellies or walking boots. Not quite the look that Fabulous Fenella the Far-Sighted had been aiming for, but when the weather turns typically British, you are obliged to adapt.

A glance up at the sky told me the drizzle was in for the evening. Now seemed a great time to be heading back to my caravan to cosy up with one of the books I'd brought to keep myself company. First though, I'd grab some pakoras to have with my dinner.

I joined the queue at the Indian stall. They were already doing good business and I had to wait to order. The man in front of me, slightly taller than me, and wearing a leather jacket, a battered old fedora and dirty denim jeans looked from behind like an archetypal hippie. In profile I could see he was wearing a tie-dye t-shirt and several strings of wooden beads. The boots on his feet were old army surplus, worn and well-lived in. He turned slightly and caught me staring at him, smiled absently, then turned to face the front once more.

I stared at the back of his head in puzzlement. Could I be seeing things? The set of his shoulders was the giveaway. Upright, straight, pulled back. I watched him move forwards and I knew I was right.

I tapped him on the shoulder and he turned back to me, ready to smile once more, perhaps expecting to exchange pleasantries.

"George?" I asked incredulously.

His eyes widened in alarm, but also confusion. He didn't know me from Adam after all.

"What are you doing here?" I hissed, keeping my

voice quiet. Nonetheless other people in the queue were glancing our way in interest.

He shook his head, a warning to me—whomever I might be—not to say anything else.

"Do I know you?" he asked. There was no recognition is his face at all. "I think we may have a case of mistaken identity here."

Not for me. It was definitely him. I'd recognise his dulcet tones anywhere.

I leant closer to him, a mere inch or so away from his lips.

"It's Alf, you dolt," I whispered. Then I kissed him.

CHAPTER FIVE

Thirty minutes later we were sitting cross-legged on the bunk in my caravan tucking into an Indian feast. Gobi Mussallem, Tofu Butter Masala, Bombay potatoes and peas, rotis, pakoras and rice. Delicious and filling, and the perfect meal for such a miserable evening.

"I can't get over you looking like this," George said for the umpteenth time, and I laughed and scooped up some sauce with a piece of roti. My fingers were turning yellow from the turmeric.

"It's a far superior disguise to yours," I said pointedly. Now that he'd removed the fedora, I could see that he'd gone to the trouble of having his head shaved. "The tattoos are impressive though." He'd had some dye applied to his scalp and arms that gave the impression he was covered in Celtic tattoos. They looked surprisingly good on him. The green contact lenses were a step too far though. I was used to his grey-blue eyes. Green on him was just wrong.

"Was it painful?" he asked.

"No." I thought back to my afternoon with Cordelia the Cosmetic Alchemist in Bristol. "Not at all. It was a bit like I imagine getting a spray tan must feel. Lots of soft brushes, and things being squirted at me." I pummelled a cushion next to me, careful not to wipe my fingers on the fabric. "If you can imagine it like a deep tissue massage, with someone prodding and poking and pulling, that about sums it up. The most painful aspect of the whole procedure was when my hair changed. That kind of felt like someone was pulling it out by the roots. It made my eyes water, I can tell you."

George grimaced. "Eww. You're a braver person than I am. I just had Stacey from the emergency call centre at work help me with the tattoos. I raided the charity shop for the clothes. Well apart from the leather jacket. This one belonged to my Dad. He was a biker in the seventies."

I laughed in delight. "I never knew that about your Dad."

"Truth."

I pointed at his head, wondering who Stacey was. "Quite a radical new hairstyle."

"I needed something completely different from my normal style otherwise I would have had to wear a wig and I didn't really fancy that." He shook his head at me. "I can't get over yours either."

"A sleek, black bob? I know. I was pretty speechless when I first saw myself in the mirror."

George laughed and began tidying up the plates. "I know it's you because I can hear it is, but you look so different."

"Older," I lamented.

"Yes older, and somehow... well your look is fitting for the character of Fenella the fortune teller, put it that way." He sounded doubtful.

"But?"

He placed the bowls and cutlery in the washing up bowl. There was no sink in the caravan, so we would have to carry them outside to the temporary wash stand that had been set up, in order to clean up. I didn't fancy tramping back out into the damp weather. I just wanted to snuggle into the cushions.

George turned to face me. "You're not my Alf, when you look all sleek and sophisticated and mysterious."

"Is that right?"

"My Alf is fuzzy and frizzy and soft around the edges, and open and funny and feisty."

My face fell. "So you don't like Fenella then?"

"Scootch over," George instructed, and I made room for him on my bunk, "And let's find out."

Later, wrapped in blankets against the chill of the evening, with the washing up done and everything stowed neatly away, we sat on the step of the caravan and watched people coming and going around the camp. A few fires had been lit around the field, and shadowy figures hunched around those. The faint smell of barbeques scented the air.

George, being a policeman, was adept at watching people closely and observing things even when he looked preoccupied. I watched him watching everyone else, trying to pick up some tips.

"So when you said you were going away, you meant you would be here undercover," I whispered, and he nodded.

"I couldn't tell you."

"Weren't you worried I'd spot you?"

"I didn't think you'd be able to see through my cunning disguise if I'm honest."

I laughed loudly and a few other folks looked our way and smiled.

George pouted playfully, and I thumped his arm. "And besides, you were barred. You told me that."

True.

"I suppose if people don't know you as well as me, and they weren't looking too closely, they wouldn't recognise you," I relented.

"Good." George turned his attention back to the camp.

"What are you looking for, anyway?" I asked quietly.

His eyes, strangely coloured with the green contact lenses, regarded me thoughtfully. "You know I can't really talk about it."

"That's cool," I said, nudging him with my shoulder. "Confidentiality and all that. I get it."

He nodded. "Seeing as it's you though. Swear to me you won't breathe a word to anyone."

"On Mr Hoo's life," I said.

"We had a tip off about some dodgy dealing. A big gang, who've started operating out of Plymouth, who are flooding the whole of the south west with their products. Some of these products are, shall we say, extremely dangerous."

I grimaced. "Not nice."

"Oh that's not the worst of it." George glanced around. "They've encroached on another gang's territory. A family whom we've been aware of for decades. I mean, real bad'ns historically. A legacy handed down over the generations. Like the Kray family, you know?"

"Oh," I said. You might have imagined that living in a rural paradise came without much in the way of crime, but George always seemed to be busy.

"There's potential for a real blood bath, so we're keeping our eyes peeled."

"You think they're here?" I looked around at the tents and caravans, eyes wide at the idea of dangerous criminals among the psychic fraternity.

George sighed, and shrugged. "They could be anywhere. But... yeah, we received some intelligence that they were."

"From whom?"

George grinned. "I certainly can't tell you that, can I?"

I laughed, "I suppose not."

"What about you?" he asked, dropping his voice to a conspiratorial whisper once more. "Why have you gone to all this trouble, with this amazing caravan and the whole makeover? It must be important. You've had the full works."

I huddled up closer to him, my lips brushing his cheek. "This is all Wizard Shadowmender's idea. He thinks The Mori are operating here in Whittle-combe, probably at the Fayre, and he wants me to see if I can find any leads."

George considered what I'd said. We had discussed The Mori previously, in relation to the death of Derek Pearce. He knew about Jed. I'd told him about the spinning globes, particularly the one I'd found in Derek Pearce's cottage. Any other detective might have had a hard time believing some of my incredulous stories and crackpot theories, but George knew I was a witch, enjoyed the company of the ghosts at Whittle Inn and had even met the vampires I'd entertained as guests in the lead up to Halloween. He found nothing incredulous any more. It made things so much easier for me.

The only problem we had was that he was one detective on a police force that would not have held much truck with a highly secretive organisation of warlocks such as The Mori. If he had run to them with my theories, he'd have been laughed out of the force.

"I'm not sure I like the idea of you doing that," he said eventually. "From everything you've told me, they strike me as incredibly dangerous. You could end up in all sorts of trouble."

"I don't like it much either. But I couldn't turn

Wizard Shadowmender down, not after everything he has done for me. And look at all the trouble he went to." I indicated the caravan and my new sleek self. "This took a lot of work. So you and I had better look out for each other."

"We had."

"Where are you staying anyway?" I asked, scanning the field for a likely tent. I suppose I was looking for something practical and expensive. Something that would stand up to the vagaries of March winds and rainy weather. When George pointed at a sunken shape in the centre of the field I struggled to see it in the shadows at first, until he told me to count three in and three down. I did a double take. His tent was tiny, the sort of thing one man might unroll from his backpack and huddle into on the side of a mountain. He'd barely be able to sit up in it. No doubt it would be capable of keeping a stiff breeze out, but only if the whole thing didn't blow away first.

"You are joking?" I giggled.

"What's wrong with it?"

"A stiff westerly and you'll find yourself flying over the hill to Abbotts Cromleigh," I said. "If you don't get snagged in the trees first."

"Oh. Haha." George wasn't amused. "Cost me an arm and a leg that thing."

It couldn't possibly have done. It looked like a plastic rag. "You know what? Maybe you'd better stay with me. There's room," I suggested, but George was adamant that we should each have our own space. I kissed him goodnight and he headed over to his little camp. I couldn't help laughing, watching him clambering into the narrow entrance, wriggling like a caterpillar. When he was safely inside, I made myself comfortable in my luxurious caravan, snuggling down beneath the quilt, surrounded by soft pillows, listening to the light rain spatter against the window.

I was asleep in no time.

CHAPTER SIX

The next morning dawned bright and sunny although the winds were high, and thick white clouds scudded across the sky at a brisk rate. I was awake early but even so many of the other campers were already up and about. I could hear people chatting and laughing and calling out to each other as the field began to get itself ready for the day, the scent of sizzling bacon all-pervading.

There was an air of expectancy everywhere. Today the Fayre would be officially launched. I dressed myself in my new midnight blue robes and paid special attention to my make-up. I wanted to look smouldering and mysterious. What had George called me?

Oh yes.

Fuzzy and frizzy and soft around the edges.

No, today I was Fenella, far sighted ice-maiden,

sleek and sure-footed, mean, moody and magnificent.

I carefully extricated my scrying orb from its box and twisted it to the light. The last time I'd utilised it, I'd been shown how to reach the entrance to the Fae Fortress, beyond Mara's the Stormbringer's cabin in the woods. At that time, the orb had resembled a snow globe and a star had appeared to lead me in the right direction. I waited for the clouds to settle, the orb glowing with a soft energy, colours twirling within the glass.

As I gazed into the orb, I began to make out shapes. A cloth of green became a field. The field where the Fayre had been set up. Little colourful splodges became sharper, and honing into view were The Hay Loft, Whittle Stores and the post office. Behind them, I could make out the village green and the pond. I turned the orb around, looking at the scene from every angle, and smiled to see a teeny-tiny Stan organising his neat vegetable stand outside his beloved shop.

Pleased to find the orb working, at least in some sense, I dusted off the glass and tucked it under my arm, wondering whether it would help me tell fortunes or not. It worried me that it wouldn't, but I could only trust in Wizard Shadowmender. I skipped out of the caravan ready to face the day, joining the merry throng of stall-holders, psychics, fortune tellers and all, as they made their way into the main field.

I spotted the BBC camera crew again. Kylie Griffiths and her sound recordist with the enormous furry microphone, and the bearded cameraman. Perhaps they were preparing for an in-depth look at the Fayre and the people involved.

Whatever.

I had no desire to appear on TV. You never knew who might be watching and who might be able to see through my disguise. I didn't want to risk it.

I went with the flow, meandering down to the huge gate at the front of the field where the main entrance to the Fayre had been located, smiling at Kahlila when I passed her, and waving at Morton, standing a head taller than anyone else. A new ticket booth had been set up, and landlord Lyle had hired a young woman to take admission fees and give out tickets. A ribbon acting as a barrier, had been tied to each gate post.

Wondering how he'd slept in his fun-size tent, I looked about for any sign of George. Instead I spotted Lyle Cavendish himself, and my old adversary Gladstone Talbot-Lloyd huddled together with a small dark-haired man I vaguely recognised although initially I couldn't place where I knew him from.

I moved purposefully down the field until I could stand around twenty or so feet away. I couldn't hear what they were saying but I had a clearer view.

The dark-haired chap looked up for a moment, laughing at a joke Gladstone Talbot-Lloyd had shared. Now I could see his face more clearly, I realised I knew him as a TV doctor. When I'd been working in London, I'd seen him on national programmes, usually in the morning. He sat in on phone-ins, advising viewers about their various health conditions. Perhaps he was a local celebrity. I knew there were a few living in the area. He appeared to be wearing quite a bit of make-up—most remarkably a shed-load of fake tan—and his hair was much darker than you would expect for someone his age. Mutton dressed as lamb—I surmised.

It transpired that Dr Alan Vaughan had been invited to the opening, expressly with the intention that he would cut the ribbon and officially open the Fayre. He gave the media something else to focus on and therefore loaned the event a certain amount of kudos, although I couldn't see the link between medicine and fortune telling to be fair.

I mingled among the stallholders on my side of

the ribbon and listened as Lyle gave a little speech welcoming everyone to Whittlecombe, turning a little pink-cheeked when he stumbled over his words. He wasn't a natural speaker, our Lyle, and I had to hide a smirk. Talbot-Lloyd stood behind him, ostensibly to encourage him, a half-smile playing on his lips, but I could see the tension in his shoulders every time Lyle made a mess of his words.

No matter. Lyle quickly wrapped up his speech and handed over to Dr Vaughan, who was much more accomplished and smooth-talking. He posed for pictures, both of the still lens camera variety, and for Kylie and her team, and then mimed cutting the ribbon several times, as cameras and phones clicked and flashed around him.

Finally, the time had come. "I'd like to reiterate what my good friend Lyle Cavendish has said and welcome you all to Whittlecombe and The Hay Loft. I'm sure you'll have the most wonderful time here. I now declare the First Annual Whittlecombe Psychic and Holistic Convention open for business." With a flourish, Dr Vaughan cut through the ribbon, and then, as a brass band struck up a cheerful tune, the assembled masses on the other side of the fence spilled into the field with a loud cheer.

I gaped in astonishment at the waiting crowd.

Hundreds of people were waiting patiently in a good old British queue to hand over their cash at the ticket office, and dozens of cars were lined up waiting to pull into the car-park's entrance. I don't think I'd seen as many people in one place since moving from London.

Somehow, Lyle had achieved the impossible. He had found a way to lure people into our rural part of the world. Instead of a village fete that perhaps a few hundred might choose to visit, he had managed to attract thousands. I couldn't be sure where all these visitors were coming from, but they had to be from further afield. Durscombe, Abbotts Cromleigh, Honiton, maybe even Exeter and beyond. It was an impressive turnout.

They scurried in, excited to see what the Fayre offered. Some made their way straight for the food stalls, others went in search of readings or castings. Many ran for the fairground rides. I stood rooted to the spot as people drifted past me. How would I find any evidence of The Mori among the sheer number of people gathering here?

It seemed Wizard Shadowmender had given me an impossible task.

Returning to my own booth after a tentative wander around the field, I spotted someone outside. Hurrying to join them, with the expectation that it might be my first willing victim, waiting to grab a reading from me, I was somewhat taken aback to see Kahlila there, rattling the door.

"Hi," I said.

She jumped when I spoke to her and twisted around to face me. "Oh hello, Fenella." She flushed a little pink, and I frowned. She avoided my eyes by looking at her shoes.

I hadn't been particularly perturbed to find her there, maybe she was looking for me after all, but her obviously guilty expression perplexed me. "Were you looking for me?" I prompted.

"Yes, yes," she said, her words tumbling forwards in a breathy rush. "I thought maybe you'd like to join me for a cup of tea and a chinwag?"

I nodded. *Is that what you were really up to? How odd.*

A couple of teenage girls chose that moment to approach her booth and read her sign. "It looks like you might have some customers." I nodded across to her pitch.

The look of relief on Kahlila's face was unmistakeable. "Laters then? Yeah?" She scrambled away, engaging the girls in friendly conversation in no time,

Hmm.

I checked the door of my booth. Still secure. I decided that for the duration of the Fayre, I'd probably be wise never to leave the orb unsecured.

I suppose I could have taken the opportunity to open my own booth and sit there as Fabulous Fenella, offering readings there and then, but I wanted to explore the Fayre, the stall holders, and the attendees in a little more depth. I figured that hiding in plain sight—by which I mean mingling with the crowd—might be the best way to go about it. And so it was that I went from stall to stall, booth to booth and food-stop to food-stop, putting Kahlila out of my mind.

I found that by going with the flow and tagging on behind a small crowd I could listen in to a variety of conversations from all sides. Most of the people streaming through the gates were here for the spectacle, and obviously there were a couple of big pulls. The voodoo high priestess from New Orleans was one of these.

Mama Henri, as she was known, had one of the largest tents on the field. In fact, it was more of a double marquee than a single tent and it had been ornately decorated with a variety of colourful props. I could see feathers, shells and animal heads strung up, among the dark coloured bunting. I joined a queue of people waiting patiently to go inside.

The marquee itself was in two parts. Peeking through to the main section I could see several lines of benches arranged on the grass floor and a small raised stage with what looked like a craved throne in the centre. But here, this first section acted as a kind of shop, beautifully arranged with rustic-looking shelving, freestanding but weighted, in case of adverse weather conditions no doubt.

The shelves carried a large range of jewellery, charms and bottled potions. On closer inspection I could see the jewellery consisted largely of amulets, or gris-gris as they were known, along with a wide range of charms. Small paper packets of magical powders and prettily wrapped sachets were hand-labelled as spells, the writing small and neat. Each of these were guaranteed to cure ailments, grant your desires, or confound one's enemies.

I turned a couple of these packages over in my hands for a while, wondering what they contained and whether I could make use of them against The Mori. I felt that an audience with Mama Henri might not be a bad idea.

At the entrance of the marquee was a small table, where a young man, brightly dressed in an impressive red silk suit with bright yellow stripes, and a matching top hat, was taking bookings and organising Mama Henri's schedule.

I tagged behind a couple of highly excitable young women who were chatting with him. They appeared crestfallen when they heard the high-end price of a one-to-one with the Priestess herself, and I had to admit it seemed a lot to fork out. The women in front of me instead opted for the much cheaper 'show' tickets. It transpired Mama Henri was doing fifteen-minute shows at regular intervals throughout the day, to select audiences of about twenty people at a time, in addition to her private slots. I figured I'd book in to watch the show later in the week and see what all the fuss was about.

I started to move away when the young man in the bright suit clocked me. He did a double take and held eye contact for longer than was comfortable. I tried to look away, but he compelled me to stare back at him as he read my face, his brow creasing in thought. I thought he would say something, but he suddenly seemed to think better of it. Unsure of his thoughts, I decided to beat a hasty retreat and sidestepped a few dawdlers at the exit so I could make my way through. Glancing back I could see he was still watching me, but then he disappeared into the inner marquee and was lost from my sight.

What was that about?

Did he know me?

There was a time when I would have said that any witch will recognise another of his or her kind without too much difficulty. While living in London I had frequently recognised both friends and foes while using public transport or when they visited the clubs, pubs and hotels I had worked in.

All that had changed when I had met Jed. How had I not recognised what he was?

I'd been well and truly hoodwinked.

With my thoughts attuned to Jed, a flash of red in the corner of my eye had me spinning around and gasping. *The Mori?* I swivelled about, but it was just a little girl in a red anorak. I laughed inwardly, figuring I might be losing the plot?

I pulled myself together and spent another thirty or so minutes following the herd from booth to booth, tent to tent. Some of the attractions—if that's what you wanted to call them—were interesting. I'd been wrong to tar everyone with the same brush when I'd dismissed the Fayre in discussion with Charity. There were people here who had a genuine gift.

I spotted the man mountain doing simple rune readings at a foot-high table in the open air. Morton perched on a tiny stool, and had each customer sit opposite him. They were instructed to draw out three runes from a bag and place them on the table. Morton then gave them a brief rundown of the meaning of each rune and suggested a potential joined-up meaning. He managed to do all of this without being overly specific or prescriptive, and his customers appeared happy enough with the results.

I joined the small crowd around him, and when he spotted me he lifted one of his huge arms and waved. "Alfanella," he called, and I grimaced inwardly. He was obviously one of those people who forgot nothing. "Let me do a little casting for you."

I wanted to protest, but people moved out of my way to allow me closer. A young woman relinquished her low stool so that I could join Morton at the table. He handed me a small hessian sack, heavy with the weight of the stones inside.

"Have a rummage," he instructed, "and then place three down on the table in front of you."

I did as he asked, moving the stones around in the pouch, feeling them slipping through my fingers, finally curling my hand around one. I hooked it out and lay it on the table, following the same process for the second and third stone, before handing the pouch over to Morton.

He hunched over the table and studied the runes carefully. Then looked up at me. "An interesting combination," he announced, running a stubby finger underneath the stones. "This one is Hagalaz." He pointed at the stone with what looked like an H carved into it. "It refers to the destructive forces of nature, and things that are out of your control. Generally I would advise that you should 'go with the flow' as you say in English. Swim with the tide."

He stabbed at the second stone. "Then there is this. This is Ansuz. Ansuz in this case is reversed. It is a warning." I looked at the F symbol, lying the wrong way around. "It tells you to watch out for trickery, or to look to the dark side of yourself. It can be a failure in communication. Are you communicating freely, Alfanella?"

His eyes glittered as he regarded me with interest. For the second time that morning I sensed that my disguise was not all it could be. I understood from Morton's look he recognised there was something odd or different about me.

"And the third one?" I asked, holding his gaze, silently protesting my innocence.

He plucked the stone from the table. A symbol

like a letter R. "This is Raidho. And again, it is reversed. It suggests you will embark on an unexpected journey – and again, we have the inference of dropped communication."

"What does all that mean?" I asked, frowning. "It doesn't sound very good for me."

"It certainly sounds like a challenge," the mountain man agreed.

I reached for my purse, but Morton wagged a finger at me. "On the house," he said. "But Alfanella, the stones have spoken. You take very good care now."

I smiled to reassure him, thanked him for his generosity and pushed my way through the crowd. I paused, standing on the periphery, watching him with his next customer, ruminating on whether he was genuine or not.

Destruction and trickery? Failed communication? A journey?

None of that sounded fun.

I broke away from the group and wandered slowly among the sideshows, trying to distract myself from my despondency by watching kids throwing balls at a coconut shy, and then trying my luck at 'Hook-a-duck', before turning to the main drag and examining the other skills on offer among the attendees.

If Morton was the real deal, other attractions certainly provided more trickery. I noted several crystal ball gazers, and of course, while I couldn't get inside their tents while they were doing their readings, I wasn't entirely convinced by their demeanour or by their equipment. People are easily fooled by an element of theatre, and this was a useful lesson for me to learn.

The rumbling of my stomach took me by surprise. I hadn't realised how much time had flown. I about-faced and headed back to the entrance and the catering vans parked there. It was time to find out more about the local sausage seller.

The sausage van had opened for business and started pulling in punters. As soon as I could see the gentleman frying his bangers, I recognised the owner by sight. Rob Parker. He lived with his wife, Debbie, in one of my tied cottages. Sparrow Cottage had once been the home of Florence's beau, Thomas Gilles. Since finding out about him I'd often wondered whether any trace of him—or of Marjorie Denby, whom according to my housekeeper at least, had been a shrewish Baptist—had remained in the cottage.

I hadn't really had much to do with Rob and Debbie up until now. They were quiet people, as most folk in the village tended to be, who kept themselves to themselves. Their little cottage and garden were immaculate, and I'd had no reason to trouble them, or they me. I hadn't realised that Rob owned a sausage business. I wondered where he kept his van as I'd never seen it on Whittle Lane—not that there would have been room for it.

When it was my turn to order, I beamed at him and was just about to introduce myself as his land-lady when I remembered I was Fabulous Fenella and he wouldn't recognise me. Not for the first time, I cursed my disguise.

"How're you doing?" he asked, which loosely translated as, 'what can I do for you?'

I perused the hand-written chalk board above his head. You had three basic options: sausages with bread (either as a posh hot dog or a sausage sarnie); bangers and mash - with or without gravy; or sausage and chips - with or without gravy. There were potential side orders, of peas (mushy, processed or garden), beans, or cheese.

But it was the sheer range of available sausages that really wowed me. Pork and leek, pork and caramelised onion, pork and cider, Cumberland, beef and mustard, beef and horse radish, pork and sage, pork with sweet chilli and mango, venison, chorizo pork, pork and pepper, pork and garlic, gluten free and vegetarian. All—apart from the latter —made with quality and locally sourced Devon meats.

I opted for a posh hot dog, and while I waited for my order, struck up a conversation with Rob. "Are you local?" I asked, knowing full well he was, of course.

"I am as it happens. Just live around the corner." He flipped a row of sausages sizzling on the grill, then agitated his frying onions in a big pan. The succulent scent of the sausages was making my mouth water.

"It's such a sweet little village," I enthused.

"Yeah, it's a great place to live."

Rob served me an enormous pork banger with a pile of onions. I helped myself to a smidge of mustard and a large dollop of ketchup along with several napkins. The logo on the napkins said, "Parker's Porky Perfection."

Rob caught me studying them. "Oh, I ran out of

the one's that match the branding on this van. I have another van. I use the other one for dirt track meets, football matches, things of that nature. Then I use this one for slightly more upmarket events." I bet he charged more for the products he sold from this van.

I raised my eyebrows. *Two vans?* "Not a lot of room to park a van this size, I wouldn't have thought. Let alone two. Not in these little narrow lanes."

"That's true. You're hard pushed to park a car around here unless you have a drive, let alone this great thing." Rob patted the counter and glanced around the van fondly. He was obviously proud of it. "I have a lock-up, not far from here. I park them both there. Nice and safe."

"That's useful." *Very useful.* "Does it belong to The Hay Loft?" It was a shot in the dark.

"No, no. It's on Piddlecombe Farm. Not far from here."

"Oh," I said. I had a vague inkling I might have heard of the farm although I couldn't figure out why. In any case, it was useful information to have.

"Is that where you farm your meat?" I asked, inspecting the feast in front of me with big Alf eyes in a Fenella face. It was a shame Fabulous Fenella had such a dainty mouth.

"No, they don't have much in the way of livestock up there. The fields are mainly let to other farmers from neighbouring properties. There's some wheat and rape. A small dairy herd."

"But you do source locally?" The van said he did. Surely it was against the Trade Descriptions Act to say something that wasn't true. False pretences and all that.

"Oh yes. There's a couple of farms Honiton way, plus one or two on Dartmoor. I get some from North Devon too. There some great stock up that way."

"You must have to know a lot about the quality of meat?" I licked at the ketchup and received a blast of mustard for my trouble too. My tongue tingled.

"I used to be a butcher, so I know exactly what I'm looking for. Enjoy!" he said and turned to the person behind me who stood patiently waiting to order.

I took a big bite of sausage. It exploded in my mouth and the juices dribbled down my chin. It was a complete taste sensation: succulent, peppery, with a hint of fresh spices.

Slender Fenella was going to become Chubby Fenella quite quickly.

Fabulous.

CHAPTER SEVEN

L oitering around the Fayre didn't produce any tangible results, although I did get to know a few more of the stallholders, psychics and seers. Nonetheless, the following day I decided I couldn't put it off any longer. It was time to open my own booth and set to work with my orb.

Essentially my booth consisted of a small garden shed with a stable door, that had been painted in midnight blue to match my new robes. Inside, Wizard Shadowmender had arranged for some refurbishment to make it look a little more the part. How he had achieved this from a distance I had no idea. But the man was a wonderful wizard, you had to give him that.

The bare wooden walls of the booth had been covered with thick navy gossamer curtains, threaded with sparkles and beads. Fairy lights decorated the window and the ceiling, and a couple of cheap imitation art deco style lamps had been placed on side tables to add mood lighting. A circular rug had been arranged on the floor beneath a round plastic garden table. This in turn had been thoughtfully covered with a navy-blue cloth, and three garden chairs were arranged around it. There really wasn't much room for anything else.

Moon and stars bunting fluttered in the wind, hanging around the outside of the shed, and three smart wooden signs, neatly hand painted, had been tacked to the wood. One of these grandly announced me as 'Fabulous Fenella the Farsighted' in large letters, and the other broadcast the legend: 'Seer of extraordinary things. Step inside for an insight into your future.' The final sign outlined my prices. I would be charging £15 for a twenty-minute reading apparently.

Fair enough.

I pulled the orb from my bag and set it on a square of velvet, then gave it a good polish. It caught the light and sparkled excitedly. Meanwhile my heart fluttered in my chest. What if I couldn't find anything in the orb to share with my clients? What if all I saw was doom and gloom? There was no way I would feel able to share bad news.

Or what if the orb was nothing more than a glorified snow globe and the only thing I saw was snow and the cabin in the woods where the Good Witch Mara resided?

Someone at the front of the field shook an old hand bell. This sound had become the signal to announce the opening and closing of the Fayre each day. I watched as scores of people tumbled into the field and quickly dispersed among the stalls, booths and food wagons, or headed for the fun fair.

I settled into my chair. It wasn't particularly comfy. Fenella didn't have a great deal of padding of her own, to be fair. Not to worry. Perhaps nobody would be interested in what I had to offer, and I'd have the opportunity to head back to the caravan for a cushion, or maybe go in search of a late breakfast instead.

But no.

"Oh, it's open today," said a familiar voice. "That's great." The booth darkened as the owner of the voice peered in through the door. "Hi there?" she exclaimed brightly.

Rhona from the village shop.

Noooooooooo!

Of all the people I had to see first. This could be the end of a very sweet friendship.

"Hello," I responded, faking a smile. "Would you like a reading?" I hoped desperately she would be put off by the price, or maybe just change her mind, but she nodded with enthusiasm.

"Yes please. I've always wanted my fortune read by crystal ball."

Reluctantly I opened the bottom half of the door to allow Rhona in. She practically skipped across the threshold. I closed the bottom door and then pushed the upper section to, leaving a small gap so that people could see I had someone with me. Then I noticed a sign on the back. *'Reading in progress'* it announced, *'Please be patient'*. I slipped the sign on to a hook on the front of the door and indicated that Rhona should take a seat.

I took my place opposite her, my breath ragged in my tight throat. I coughed, and Rhona looked me over with concern. Fortunately, she didn't seem to recognise me at all. My cosmetic alchemy was obviously working well among non-psychics.

"Sorry," I said, "I'm a little bit wheezy from all the camp fires." I dropped my shoulders and took a deep breath, closing my eyes for a moment and centring myself. When I opened them again, focusing on the orb, smoke began to swirl in its depths. My stomach lurched.

I leaned over the table, gazing intently into the glass. Rhona did the same. We were quiet, and I briefly wondered whether the silence was going on too long. For now though, I had nothing to say because the orb wasn't showing me anything.

Nothing at all.

"It's a lot of mist, isn't it?" I laughed, nerves jangling. Rhona giggled in response also sounding a little worried, and that helped me focus. As far as my clients were concerned, they would assume I knew what I was doing. In that sense, I had the position of power. It was my responsibility to help Rhona relax.

I knew Rhona well. It would be easy for me to spiel out a load of things I knew and make it sound freaky and mysterious, but precisely because I knew her, I decided not to do that. I owed it to her to be a better person than that.

Finally the mist began to clear, and I watched, almost as entranced as Rhona. I saw her little shop and marvelled at its miniature perfection, almost forgetting to tell her.

"Do you see anything?" Rhona asked breathily, studying my face.

"Your shop," I blurted. "I see it, fully stocked." I watched as people flooded towards it. The roof of the little building shimmered with gold. "Lots of customers." I decided I probably needed to do a little lateral translation of what I was seeing. "I don't know if you've had some worries about finance, but this seems to suggest that you will do better."

Either that or you need a new roof. Why was it glowing with gold unless the symbolism referred directly to money?

"That's good news," said Rhona pleased.

The image in the orb changed. Became purple. A deep, rich reddy-purple which Rhona could see too. "What's that?" she asked, glancing around, perhaps to see if something could be causing the orb to change colour in this way.

At first I couldn't make out what I was seeing, but then almost as if we were looking at a film and the camera operator had changed the depth of vision, the camera pulled away and I was looking at aubergines. Dozens and dozens and dozens of what our US cousins call eggplants.

"Aubergines," I said in wonder.

"Aubergines?"

I waited to see if the orb would tell me more. I saw the front of the shop again, where Stan and Rhona kept a display of their vegetables. The orb kept pulling me back to the basket containing the aubergines, and then switching to strings of garlic before finally settling on lemons, and coming back to aubergines, where it lingered interminably.

"Aubergines, garlic, lemons."

The roof of the shop glowed gold again and I decided to risk my interpretation. "I think you need to buy lots."

"Well I usually have some of each in stock..."

"I mean *really* lots." I peered into the orb again but there wasn't anything else to see. Why would it be telling us about aubergines? "In fact... fill up your stock room."

Rhona laughed, her head shaking with disbelief. "You know, aubergines tend to get soft quite quickly if they're not kept correctly?"

"I know," I said. "You're just going to have to put your faith in me with this."

"Okay." Rhona smiled. She was such a genuine, trusting person. I hoped with all my heart I was offering the correct advice here.

The orb cleared and sparkled with a silvery light as though it were waiting for more instructions. It didn't have anything else to show me though. I worried that I might have short changed Rhona. What had she received in return for her tenner? I picked up the glass ball and held it out to her.

"You can ask it a question," I said. "Just hold it

up and look into it and ask it one question. It will show me the answer."

Rhona reached out tentatively and took the orb from me. She looked surprised. "It's much heavier than I imagined it would be."

"Try and keep your mind clear so you're only asking one question and look deep into the ball," I instructed. "You don't need to ask out loud. I'll tell you what I see."

She nodded. I watched her face turn serious, then she almost glared into the ball for a few seconds, blinked and handed it back to me.

The mist in the orb shimmied and spun, becoming increasingly grey and gloomy. Then as though the sun had come out, it began to clear. I saw lots of green. I looked up at Rhona. "I see ... leaves. Trees. The forest?" Rhona looked perplexed, and no wonder. Whittlecombe was a village surrounded by thick forest. I tried again, waiting for the orb to show me more. "Water." I watched as the water flowed gently down a hill, among the trees. This had to be the forest surrounding Whittlecombe. "A spring? No. A small river." I paused. The water pooled. A puddle, then something wider and deeper. And now I recognised the spot where people from the village liked to swim. Three hundred or so metres beyond

Whittle Folly. The local kids loved it there in the summer. A calm place to cool off.

Then the image changed abruptly, and I saw Stan in bed. A hospital bed. He didn't look well. I frowned. This was exactly what I had been afraid of. I didn't want to offer doom-laden fortunes to people paying me money.

"Rhona," I began, and she looked startled. *She hadn't offered me her name.* "The crystal ball has given me a warning." I tried to be gentle but that's difficult when you are trying to avoid giving somebody bad news.

"You should tell Sta—I mean, your husband—to stay away from the rock pool behind Whittle Folly."

Rhona gasped, her eyes wide with horror. "Why?" she demanded.

"I don't rightly know." A miserable sinking sensation pulled on my insides. "It's just what I'm seeing."

Rhona took a deep breath. "I see." She reached for her purse and for a moment I considered refusing her money, but then I remembered I was undercover and therefore I needed to act the part I was here to play.

"Thank you," I said as she lay her notes on the table. She offered me a tight smile, her face pale, and turned to go.

"It was just a warning," I said gently. "Make sure he takes care."

"I will." She tried to laugh, but it sounded a little forced. "And I'll stock up on aubergines."

"Lots of them," I repeated. With my stomach lined in lead, I watched her as she walked away.

Fortunately for me, following Rhona the next few readings were with people I didn't know and were entirely more straightforward. I offered advice to one older lady about her cat—to have it checked for diabetes—and then helped a gentleman find his wife's wedding band—lodged between their mattress and the headboard.

I had started to consider lunch options when my next client tapped on the door. I recognised her immediately. Sally McNab-Martin was a friend of Millicent's. Sally was an active member of the local WI and referred to by some of the locals as 'a bit of a toff'. What they meant was that Sally was well-to-do. She owned one of the large houses set back off Whittle Lane—sat prettily in its own vast grounds, spoke with a plummy accent, and drove a little silver sports car too fast around the lanes. At one stage I had fancied her as a potential member of The Mori, or at least someone who was in league with them, but now I was not so sure.

Sally, immaculately turned out as always, was nervy. She perched on the edge of the seat, with her handbag tightly squeezed to her chest, her knuckles turning white where she gripped it. Beneath the foundation and blusher covering her face, I could see how taut her jaw was. When I regarded her more closely, I noted the frayed collar of the pale blue sweater she was wearing.

Appearances can be deceptive. I studied Sally with new eyes. This woman was crying out for help, but it remained to be seen whether I was the one who could offer it.

In between us, the orb pulsed with a new energy. I could see many colours, a full spectrum of bruised purples, blues and black. They swirled in confusion.

I smiled in an attempt to put her at ease and handed her a silk cloth. "It helps if you touch the crystal ball," I said. This wasn't strictly true, but I wanted her to release her tight grip on her bag and relax a little. "Would you mind cleaning it with this?"

She reached for the ball, fumbling with it so much I was afraid she would drop it. As our fingers briefly touched, I could feel how icy hers were, as though blood no longer flowed in her veins to warm her through.

She wrapped the cloth around the orb and wiped it free of residual dust, returning it to its place on the table between us when I indicated she should do so. I waved my hands over the top of the orb, purely for theatrical purposes, and then peered deep into the glass. The swirling colours had slowed, and I could make out a figure.

"I see a man," I began, watching as his face twisted unpleasantly. "He's angry about something."

Sally jumped as though I had slapped her. I stopped, but she shook her head. "Go on," she urged, and pinched her lips together.

I could see this man and Sally in a house. Their house I could only assume. A big house. Lots of room. Just the two of them. He gesticulated wildly, and his mouth moved—he appeared to be shouting at her—not that we could hear the sound of course. I observed Sally cower away from him, then she took to her heels, running into a bedroom, slamming the door, and collapsing on to a bed, her face streaked with tears.

"You're incredibly unhappy," I said, moved to tears myself. I could feel her unhappiness, a deep well of emotion bubbling up from the orb. It punched me in the guts, making my heart heavy. Sadness, fear, pain, uncertainty.

He burst into the bedroom, the wooden door silently splintering near the lock. I jumped away from the orb, startled. *Could this really be her husband?* Whomever, he was a tyrant. "You have to get out!" The words erupted from me before I could think.

I stared across at Sally, horrified for her. "Sorry," I said. "It's not really any of my business, but it's what I'm seeing. What the orb is telling me." The mist swirled in the ball, drawing my attention. I looked again, watching as Sally packed a suitcase. *Good.*

"You want to," I said softly. "You want to leave." Then the mist rolled across the glass once more. When I looked up this time, I spotted a single tear run down Sally's cheek. She sat upright, proud and otherwise contained. She wiped the tear away with a thin, pale finger.

I picked up the orb and handed it to her once more. "You can ask the ball one question, and I will interpret what I see there in reply."

She took the ball from me once more, looking uncertain. She twisted the orb this way and that, staring into its depths as though trying to scrutinise what she saw there herself.

"Clear your mind. Make sure you're only thinking of the one question otherwise you can get a mixed response."

Sally shook her hair back over her shoulders, and then gazed into the ball once more, without blinking. I could almost hear her mind working. When she had asked what she needed to, she handed the orb back to me and I looked down. Unmistakeably I picked out numbers. Tiny numbers on silver circles. They started off as miniatures, then grew in size until they filled my view, before popping. The same numbers repeated over and over again.

"5000, 5000, 5000, 5000."

She looked at me blankly.

"That's what I see," I explained. "Those same numbers."

"What can that mean?" she asked.

I stared at the threadbare neckline of her sweater, remembered the battered suitcase I had seen her packing just moments before. What if the reason she remained with a man who frightened her so, was that—in spite of appearances, in spite of the jazzy silver sports car and the big house, the well-to-do accent and the expensive clothes—this poor woman simply had no income of her own. Perhaps she had no financial means to start a new life from scratch.

"I think it means you should go and buy a lottery ticket," I said.

After an emotionally fraught day in which I'd seen fourteen clients, I was about ready to put my feet up. I wondered whether I'd be able to track down George and maybe we could treat ourselves to some more of Parker's Porky Perfect bangers and share a bottle of wine.

Ah the high life.

Outside, the sun had begun to drop in the sky and the evening was cooling. I dusted the orb of fingerprints and smudges, wrapped it in a cloth and snuggled it into its box. Then I stood and stretched, my neck and shoulders clicking. With the notable exceptions of Sally and Rhona, the actual fortune telling had gone reasonably well. I'd become more adept at being mysterious, and had mastered the art of keeping a straight face and an impermeable expression.

A soft tap on the door alerted me to a newcomer.

I wanted to say I had finished for the day but that seemed rude. I was a witch after all. Witches don't stop being witches at 5 pm.

Resigned to giving another reading, I retrieved the orb from its box and called out, "Come on in. It's open." A tall slender woman, skin the colour of smooth dark chocolate, with large soft eyes to match, stepped into the booth. My jaw dropped.

"Mama Henri?" I asked. It could only have been her. She had decorated her face with smoky make-up, and her hair had been wound around her scalp in a complicated style of plaits and weaves. But it was the adornment on her body that gave it away. Dressed in multi-coloured silk, she wore several necklaces and bracelets made from beads, feathers and bones. On her fingers she sported enormous silver rings, one a huge ruby, another embellished with a tiny bird's skull. Where I expected her nails to be long and claw like, they were the biggest surprise, worn down, the skin around them cracked, dirt and blood—and possibly worse—embedded in the grooves and wrinkles.

"Yes," she replied, studying me with an intense gaze, her eyes moving around my face. "Oh that's good," she uttered in a low voice, rich and deep with a decided purr. "Very good. Josiah was right."

"Right about what?" I asked, my skin crawling a little under her scrutiny. The woman was inspecting me so closely she would be able to see every open pore or pimple on my face. I tried to duck my head away and she burst out laughing—surprisingly high-pitched for such a deep timbre of voice.

"Oh, my love," she said. Her accent spoke of the Deep South, of Jazz and Blues, of Creoles and Cajuns, of sass and rhythm, and style and vibrancy. Mostly though it spoke of darkness and the mausoleums and tombs of New Orleans cemeteries. "I'm sorry," she offered, but carried on roaring with laughter for another few seconds nonetheless.

Finally she stopped her cackling and nodded knowingly. "Cosmetic alchemy." She pronounced every syllable slowly and deliberately.

She could see through me. Literally.

"Yes, Mama Henri knows." She tapped her nose. "But cosmetic alchemy? Here in this little place?" She offered me her hand, shaking mine firmly when I took it. "Pleased to meet you."

"Fenella," I said firmly, although she knew for sure I lied.

She nodded meaningfully. "Josiah told me about you yesterday and I had hoped you'd return so I could meet you. But I know you have been busy."

Perhaps she'd been keeping an eye on me. She looked down at the orb. "May I?" she asked.

"Of course." I lifted it and handed it to her and she turned it carefully, gazing into its hidden depths. Then she shook her head and handed it back.

"I feel it pulse, like it lives. It is at once cold, and yet it is warm. It breathes in my hand. This is powerful magick indeed. And yet when I look inside I can see nothing!" She sounded disappointed.

I didn't know why that might be, but I assumed the orb only worked for certain people. Perhaps there was an element of programming there. No doubt Wizard Shadowmender would be able to cast light on that. Perhaps my magick made it work, while Mama Henri's did not?

Mama Henri continued, "We are sisters, you and I, under one sky. For what is voodoo but ritual and magick?" She pulled out a chair and sat. I joined her at the table placing the orb between us. Instantly the clouds rolled and twirled in the glass. It wanted to offer a reading.

Mama Henri saw my downward glance. "What do you see?" she asked.

Unsure, I studied the orb.

"I can make you out." I shook my head. "But it's impenetrable. I can hardly see you through the fog."

I watched a little longer. Smaller wisps of dark mist, like acrid smoke, flitted around her shape. In the orb, the miniature figure of Mama Henri held two hands up. "You're reaching out."

"To whom?" Mama Henri cocked her head with interest, watching me study what unfolded within the crystal.

I shrugged, hesitant. "To me, I think."

The inside of the orb exploded in black fog, then almost as if the air was sucked out if it, it cleared once more. It sat in its place, sparkling and clean, reflecting only the fairy lights from the window.

I stared across at Mama Henri, perplexed. "What does that mean, I wonder?"

"Did I need your help?" she asked.

"I couldn't tell."

"Perhaps you need mine." She sat forwards and regarded me once more. Close up I could see she was older than I'd imagined, maybe fifty or so. There were crow's feet around her eyes, and her skin— although supple—looked lived in. She was aging incredibly well.

"I speak to spirits," she said, her voice low. I realised that's exactly what I'd seen in the orb. The dark wisps. "They tell me things."

"What kind of things?"

"All kind of things. Some good, some not so good. They told me about you."

My breath caught in my throat. "What did they tell you?"

"You're a ghost whisperer."

I nodded. "I see ghost lights. I can call them and talk to them. I have some as friends. I used to think of them as my followers because they followed me around, but now I'm settled—" I shrugged. "They seem to be settled too."

"That's nice." She drew the word nice out, emphasising it, mocking me slightly. "A kind of ghostly domesticity."

She knew. She knew about me and the inn. I watched her carefully, on alert. She must have seen my body language change, sensed my tension, because she laughed once more, this time a more melodic chuckle.

"Lay your hackles down, *Fenella*." She smirked. "I don't mean you harm. Far from it. I recognise a kindred spirit when I see her. As I said before, we are sisters under one sky." She clasped her hands together under her chin, as though she were praying. "The spirits who seek me out are not always so nice as yours. Not so friendly. Not so domesticated. I exist on the cusp between this world and the next. I can use toxins to travel here and there, beyond the veil. I see things. I hear things."

"Alfhild," she continued, and I shivered when she used my real name, for I hadn't offered it to her. "I came to you to extend a hand of friendship, and to tell you, when you need me I will come." She stood, her long limbs graceful.

I opened my mouth to respond, but unsure what to say.

"You will know when to reach out to me, and you will know how to call me."

She pulled the door open and stepped outside. "Stay safe," she sang, and in a swirl of silk and a rattle of bones, she had gone.

CHAPTER EIGHT

The bathing facilities at the camp site were minimalist to say the least. They consisted of a couple of temporary showers, but given they were unisex, I wasn't keen. In any case the weather in Devon in March can be a bit hit and miss. I didn't relish the prospect of standing in a lukewarm shower, when the ambient temperature was around 12 degrees, especially when I had to wash my hair.

Besides, I'm a woman who loves a good soak in the tub with my fragrant bubble bath. It allows me time to think. And then there's Mr Hoo. I was missing him.

I therefore elected to sneak back to the inn early that evening after my encounter with Mama Henri. Without thinking I piled through the main entrance to the bar where I was accosted by a quizzical looking Charity.

"Good evening," she called as I headed for the stairs. "Do you have a reservation, Madam?"

I could have kicked myself. I hadn't let on to anyone at home that I would be changing my appearance. I edged into the main bar reluctantly. Several guests were enjoying a quiet drink while the soft notes of jazz music rose from the speakers.

"It's me," I hissed as quietly as possible.

Charity frowned in confusion. "I'm sorry?"

"It's me! Alf!" I repeated through gritted teeth.

Charity narrowed her eyes and looked me up and down. Of course she didn't believe me. Why would she? It wasn't just the hair and facial features, it was my height and size too. To her eyes I was an entirely different person.

"I'm the boss, you're my minion," I quipped, our old joke.

Charity ran her tongue nervously along her bottom lip.

For a second I thought she would consider what I was saying and opt to trust me, but then the shutters came down and she simply seemed cross. "You can't go upstairs unless you've checked in, Madam."

How could I persuade her?

I made a dash for the stairs and ran up them, two

at a time, with Charity hot on my heels. As I'd expected she didn't attempt to rugby-tackle me or manhandle me in any way. That was not in her nature at all. But she did call for Zephaniah. That made no difference either. Zephaniah, our chief fix-it ghost, couldn't touch me physically.

I reached the door of my private rooms and burst in triumphantly, only grinding to a halt when faced with the fierce disapproval on my great grandmother's face. She stood in the centre of my office, arms folded, glaring at me.

"Grandmama," I said, meekly altering my attitude. "How lovely to see you. I've missed you."

Charity joined us. "Sorry to disturb you, Gwyn. This woman is deluded. She thinks she's Alf."

"I *am* Alf!" I protested as Zephaniah apparated alongside me.

"You don't look anything like my great granddaughter." Gwyn shot one of her most withering glances at me.

"I've had a procedure," I argued. "Just a temporary one. It's turned me into Fenella." I made a move for the door and Zephaniah stepped between it and me. "For goodness sake, Zephaniah." I waved him away, and closed the door firmly.

Lowering my voice so that no guests would be able to overhear what I was about to say, I pointed out the window in the direction of Whittlecombe. "I'm working undercover at the Psychic Fayre," I whispered. "Wizard Shadowmender arranged this makeover for me. I've just come home for a bath."

Charity circled me, beholding me with suspicion. Zephaniah watched, slightly worried. Gwyn merely tutted loudly. "Prove it," she said.

I didn't know how to. Desperately I looked around. I popped my head around the door into my bedroom. Nothing I could use.

Nothing. As in no thing.

And that gave me the idea. I dashed over to the bedroom window and flung it open. "Mr Hoo?" I called. "Mr Hoo?"

At first I thought my voice had changed so much that he wouldn't recognise my call, but then from the direction of the forest, flying towards me on his huge wings, came the familiar round face with long ears. He soared gracefully, lifted himself up, then fluttered down on to the window sill.

"Mr Hoo." I laughed happily. "I've missed your feathery little face." I held my arm out and he hopped on it, walked along it and rubbed his face against mine.

"Hoo-oooo. Hoo ooo. Hoooo!"

"I know," I said to him. "I should have explained to you what I was doing and where I was going. That was wrong of me." I turned to face the others. "I should have told you all, but Wizard Shadowmender wanted secrecy so my hands were tied."

"I thought you were on a long romantic break with DS Gilchrist," Charity pouted. "I was imagining all romantic hearts and flowers."

"Unfortunately not." I sympathised. I decided it wasn't in George's best interests to admit he was down at the Fayre on a separate undercover operation of his own. I kept schtum about that. "Nothing quite so much fun or as pleasant. In fact, it's decidedly hard work." I rolled my head on my tired shoulders. "And so far I have more questions than answers."

"So why are you home?" Gwyn asked. "Isn't it a little risky for you to be back here?"

"Yes," I agreed. She was right. If anyone recognised me here, word might get back to the wrong people. "I just wanted a bath."

"You risked blowing your cover for a bath?" Gwyn disapproved. Of course she did.

"And thinking time," I said. "I really need some of that."

As wonderful as it was to see everyone, it was good to shut the door on them. I luxuriated in the hot water, the fragrant bergamot and lavender bubbles tickling my nose. Mr Hoo, twitting contentedly by the window, kept half an eye on me, and half an eye on what was going on outside, his head swivelling from side to side, no doubt considering supper.

At first I found myself preoccupied with Mama Henri's visit. That had been odd in the extreme. She had seen through me, even though nobody else could. She'd sought me out, ostensibly to offer her help should I need it. But what kind of voodoo assistance would I ever need, here in my little corner of East Devon?

I puzzled over whether I'd found her genuine and decided that yes, with a few reservations, I did. I'd had no sense that she could be dangerous to me, and the orb had not suggested that. And yet, perhaps the orb had been confused itself. It had only offered the murkiest of readings, and there was no doubt in my mind that Mama Henri was surrounded by the darkest of shadows.

I decided I would track her down myself tomorrow, and perhaps open up further dialogue, maybe see if she knew anything else that could help me.

And that brought me back to my current mission. Where was I?

Wizard Shadowmender had asked me to infiltrate the Fayre because he wanted information about Astutus and Lyle Cavendish. Was there a link between them and The Mori? So far I'd found out nothing useful. Of the stallholders I had spoken to, nobody seemed out of the ordinary.

But they were hardly going to hold their hands up and just admit to nefarious undertakings, were they?

No.

I chewed the inside of my cheek, mulling on what else I could do.

Two questions burned away inside my mind. Firstly, why exactly had Lyle decided to host the Fayre? What could he possibly be gaining from doing so?

And secondly, were The Mori in attendance?

It struck me that if The Mori were keeping a low profile now, it was because they wanted to. At some stage they would show their hand, and that would be when I'd gain some insight into what was going on.

For now I had to be patient. Wait and watch.

I smiled at my little feathered friend as his laser gaze picked out rodents scurrying on the lawn below.

I needed to channel my inner Mr Hoo.

I flicked through the post waiting on my desk, mainly bills and invoices, and created a pile for Charity to start working through in the morning. It appeared that I had a few birthday cards from friends in Somerset and London, and there was one envelope—familiar in its anonymity—that I pocketed and saved for later.

I couldn't stay long, but I briefly joined Charity and Florence in the warm kitchen for a cup of tea before I headed back into the cold, dark night and my eccentric and colourful caravan. Monsieur Emietter snoozed in a chair by the range, his moustaches twitching as he dreamed.

"What's the news here?" I asked.

"Nothing much," Charity said. "Oh, unless...did you hear about Sally?"

"Sally? Millicent's friend Sally McNab-Martin?" I knew full well which Sally Charity was referring to.

"Yes. She had a pay-out on one of those lottery scratch cards. £5000!"

"Did she?" I asked, inwardly smirking. "How do you know?"

"Millicent rang. Not long before you arrived here. She was in the shop chatting to Rhona when Sally came in. I know it's not a life changing amount of money, but it seems to be good news for Sally. Millicent said she was in tears."

"I hope she spends it wisely," I said, knowing she would. I made a mental note to ask her whether she would like to rent Primrose Cottage. She needed somewhere to escape to and I needed a tenant. It seemed like the perfect solution.

"Apparently she'd never bothered with the lottery before, neither the draws nor the scratch cards, but she went into Whittle Stores and bought a ticket on the off chance. Amazing."

"You never can tell, can you?" I said. "The future is a mystery." I sipped my tea, feeling mighty pleased with myself, then glanced at Florence. "Everything alright from your end?"

"Ship shape and Bristol fashion, Miss Alf," Florence smiled, wiping down the work surfaces. The kitchen smelled faintly of roast chicken and my stomach growled in empty dismay.

"Calm seas," Charity emphasised.

"That's good news. It means I don't have to worry about you guys all alone up here without me."

"Certainly not," said Charity, robust as always.

"Any unexpected guests or odd happenings?" I probed. It paid to stay on top of things.

"Just Mr Wylie," Florence said. "A nice quiet man."

I looked at Charity for confirmation. "He hadn't reserved a room, just tried us on the off chance when he realised The Hay Loft was full. That's where he normally stays apparently."

"Really?" I asked. For some reason my witch twitch was pulsing.

Charity noted my expression. "I'm sure it's entirely innocent, Alf."

"Details?"

"William Wylie. Down from somewhere near York on business. He arrived this morning and found The Hay Loft fully booked and the Fayre in progress, and decided he'd prefer the peace and quiet up here."

"What sort of business?"

Charity shook her head slowly and looked at Florence who shrugged.

"He had a briefcase," my head housekeeper offered helpfully.

I rolled my eyes. "Come on. You can do better than that."

"We haven't been snooping," Charity said folding her arms across her chest. "We don't do that to our guests."

I looked meaningfully at Florence. She gave an almost imperceptible nod.

"I need to get going," I announced. There would still be people at the Fayre and I could grab some food on the way to my caravan. Better to be hiding in plain sight than skulking around after everyone had retired for the night. That would look kind of obvious.

"Keep an eye on this Mr Wylie," I instructed Charity as I headed out the back door.

"No problem, *Fenella*. Will do," Charity called. "Feel free to pop in the next time you need a bath."

Florence giggled, and I winked at them.

"Look after my owl," I said.

I stopped by Parker's Porky Perfection on my way

through the Fayre. Rob greeted me like a long-lost friend. "A return customer," he enthused.

"Of course. Yesterday you introduced me to the best sausage I'd ever eaten," I replied truthfully, and Rob beamed with pleasure.

"One tries one's best." He had been cleaning down the cooking surfaces, and there wasn't a whole lot left, so I opted for pork and cider sausages, with onions, chips and onion gravy.

"Is it going well?" I asked.

"Very well," Rob said while the sausages sizzled between us. "There's not a huge amount of meat on offer among the food stalls. I reckon the carnivores are happy to have me here."

I laughed. That was true. The Fayre seemed to have attracted lots of hippie and bohemian style store holders, especially where the catering was concerned. It meant that punters had a wide range of vegetarian and vegan options, but not a huge amount of meat, if that was their preference.

I turned to survey the Fayre behind me. Most of the booths were closed for the evening now. Several of the sideshows and stalls remained open, selling wares to the stragglers. Only Mama Henri's marquee seemed busy.

"Much quieter at this time of the evening," I remarked, and Rob nodded his agreement.

"Late breakfast and then lunch are by far my busiest times," he said. "Everything else is a bonus."

"You haven't seen anyone hanging around or doing anything unusual, have you?" I asked. He had a good vantage point from his location, plus the van was positioned a few extra feet above ground level which helped. In his quiet times he could probably indulge in a little people-watching.

He shook his head and flipped my sausages. "Not really. Why do you ask?"

What to say? "Mm, someone tried to break into my booth last night," I lied.

"Oh I'm sorry to hear that. Did they get away with anything valuable?" Rob shook hot chips onto a tray, and then added my sausages.

"There's nothing really to steal."

"That's good then."

"It's just the damage, you know?"

"Yeah. That's a pain. I'll certainly keep an eye out now I know there are troublemakers around." He spooned gravy on to my tray.

"Thanks, I'd appreciate it." I opened my purse and offered him a note.

He took my money and handed over my change. "Probably kids."

"Probably."

Rob returned to cleaning his van. "I can mention it to the organiser if you'd like."

I quickly considered this. Did I want Lyle to become aware of Fabulous Fenella? What would that lead to?

Calm seas, Charity had said. Perhaps it was time to rock the boat.

"Good idea!" I smiled and headed back to my caravan.

CHAPTER NINE

The next morning, I found myself getting into my stride with my orb. Fabulous Fenella became ever more theatrical. It appeared, that with a little method acting, I could suggest ways my clients could improve their lives through small changes, without spreading too much doom and gloom. Fortunately for me, the orb made it easy, rarely offering anything too life-shattering or catastrophic, meaning I didn't have to ruin anyone's life, intentionally or otherwise.

But this was in sharp juxtaposition to the reading I'd performed for Rhona the previous day. As I broke for lunch I couldn't help pondering on the meaning behind her fortune. Why had the orb shown me a poorly Stan? I'd genuinely had the sense his illness was serious, and that worried me. Maybe the orb had shown me, precisely because he was my friend.

Or perhaps there was some other reason.

I grabbed my purse and swung my little wooden sign over. *'Back soon!'*

Outside, the Fayre was as busy as ever, almost as if coachloads of people were being dropped off in the village. They poured through the gates, and milled around the stalls, three or four deep in some cases.

It was just after one and I could see that Parker's Porky Perfection was doing a roaring trade. Perhaps I needed to eat something else or Fenella would transform into a sausage. A change is as good as a rest, they say. I turned right out of my booth, intent on investigating the Vietnamese soup and noodle bar, when a sudden commotion stole my attention.

A woman cried out for help, and as I swivelled to look, I caught sight of someone falling to the ground. I rushed forwards, along with several other people. An older gentleman lay face down on the grass. I reached him first and helped to gently roll him over.

"Mr Bramble!" I gasped and realised that the woman who had called out was his wife.

"He says he has chest pain," she cried, ringing her hands, her face a picture of horror. "Oh help him. Somebody please help him."

"Let me though please," came a voice I recognised.

George knelt next to Mr Bramble and quickly took the older man's pulse. "I need someone to phone 999 for me," George called, and a young woman on the other side of us fished her mobile out of her pocket, and rapidly put the call in.

"Tell them we are on the field behind The Hay Loft in Whittlecombe, and we have a gentleman with a suspected heart attack. Conscious and breathing. Erratic pulse."

The young woman relayed the information.

"It's Ernest Bramble," I told George. "He lives in Ash Cottage."

George nodded, then leaned in close to the old man, whose eyes had closed. "Stay with me, Mr Bramble." He felt for the man's pulse again.

"We're going to lose him," George said. He looked up at the girl. "Tell them to hurry. He's in a bad way. I think he's going into cardiac arrest." As he spoke the old man seemed to sink into himself and George returned his attention to the old man on the floor. "Okay. He's stopped breathing."

The girl, increasingly panicked, told the emergency operator the bad news. "They've dispatched an ambulance. Ten minutes, she thinks."

"I'm going to have to start chest compressions. Clear the way, please."

People shuffled away so that George could work. I sat back on my heels, aghast at how fate had dealt this blow to such a lovely man. George tipped Mr Bramble's head back and breathed into his mouth, watching his chest rise and fall. Once, twice. Then he began chest compressions.

I stood and reached for Mrs Bramble, holding her close in a hug as the tears streamed down her face.

"I don't want to lose him," she sobbed. "It's his birthday next week."

The ambulance arrived twenty minutes later, having had trouble getting through the traffic around the village. I supposed there had been an issue with cars parking anywhere they could find a space. It meant that larger vehicles were finding it difficult to manoeuvre around the village. The paramedics took over from George, who slumped in exhaustion, still concerned about Mr Bramble.

After another fifteen minutes working on the old man, they stabilised him well enough to risk moving him. Mrs Bramble took a moment to thank George for what he had done and then turned to follow the ambulance crew. As she walked away I spotted something on the ground where she'd been standing.

"Wait," I called. "You've dropped something." I bent down to retrieve the item. A card. I held it out to her and she took it off me.

"Oh that!" she spat in disgust hastily thrusting it back into my hands.

"What's up?" I asked, turning it over to examine it. A tarot card. The card itself was old, stained the colour of spilt tea. The colours on the image were muted, the edges well-thumbed.

"Ernest had just been in to see the tarot reader. When he came out he was very upset. Said we had to leave. Immediately. I don't know what that man said to him in there, but it caused my husband severe distress."

"Which tarot reader?" I asked, because I knew there were a few at the Fayre.

"A wooden booth towards the back of the field," she said, then dashed after the green uniformed paramedics, pushing her poorly husband on the trolley towards the blue flashing lights of the ambulance that had parked up near the gate.

George came to stand with me, rolling his shoulders, and looking a little grey around the gills.

"Are you okay?" I asked.

He smiled. "Of course. It's always a bit distressing. You know, when someone is taken ill or they get hurt. You try to help them, and then after the adrenaline fades, you realise you're a little shocked yourself."

I squeezed his arm. "You did a good thing there. He was lucky you were around." *Incredibly lucky.* Perhaps someone else would have known what to do, and maybe they would have acted as quickly. But what if...?

"I just hope he makes it."

"I've got everything crossed," I said. "Look, why don't you come to the caravan later? We'll grab some dinner from one of the food trucks and a bottle of wine or a few beers from Rhona."

"I'd like that."

"It's a deal then." I looked down at the card in my hand once more, flipping it over. Having studied the Tarot many years before, I recognised the card instantly. The Tower.

Expect the unexpected – massive change, upheaval, destruction and chaos.

"What's that?" George asked, peering over my shoulder.

"A tarot card. Mr Bramble had just had a reading

and his wife says he came out of the tent in an agitated state."

George frowned. "It must have been a bad reading."

"That would be incredibly bad form," I said, thinking guiltily of my session with Rhona.

George looked puzzled. "Isn't it a case of say what you see?"

"It's a matter of interpretation. There are any number of ways to interpret the cards. They depend in large part on how each card relates to the others in the spread. It would be unusual for a reading to only deliver bad news. The reading would be nuanced in different ways."

"I wonder what upset him then? Maybe it wasn't the reading?"

I nodded. "Maybe it was the reader."

We grabbed a couple of coffees from one of the less busy food stalls and strolled around the rear of the field. There were several stalls and booths and tents in red, but we were able to discount all of them because none of them offered tarot readings.

"This is a wild goose chase," George complained,

but I was determined to track the tarot reader down. We walked around once more, retracing our steps, until we were almost at my booth. I sighed in exasperation. George was right. We were going around in circles and getting nowhere.

I cast a glance to my left and spotted something slightly out of the ordinary. The booth next to me, so very similar to mine—little more than a small garden shed with a stable door—appeared to have been abandoned. The bottom half of the door was closed, but the top swung in the breeze. Gone were the cheerful bunting and the little signs. As the door flapped open and closed, a flash of red from inside, caught my eye.

"That's strange. Where's Kooky Kahlila?"

"Kahlila?"

"She's a shaman. She channels spirit energy to help people with problems."

"A shaman?" George plucked her A Board from where it was leaning against the shed, then turned it around so I could read it. "That's not what it says here."

"Well, well, well." *Kooky Kahlila, tarot reader to the stars.* I stared at the writing in confusion. "I swear, that's not what her board said the other day." George looked dubious. "Honestly. I had a conversation with her. She actually spelled out what she did." I copied the gesture she had made: hands circling my head, crossing my heart and dropping to the ground.

George watched me and shook his head, bemused. "Interesting. Maybe she decided she wasn't making enough money, so she bailed out of shamanism and decided to try her hand at tarot."

"She could have been proficient in both, I suppose." There was no reason why not, I just found it odd that she hadn't mentioned it when we spoke before.

I walked determinedly up to the booth before George could stop me and yanked the top half of the stable door open. Inside the booth was virtually empty. One table, much like mine, and two stools in plain wood were the only contents, apart from another A board propped against the wall.

I leaned over the door so that I could pull the latch back on the bottom half, and stepped in. George followed me, looking about us cautiously, then swivelled the board around.

"This one says, Kooky Kahlila in residence. Shaman and spiritual healer to the stars."

"There you are then. She had several irons in the fire."

"Spiritual healer to the stars? Which stars?" George pondered.

"Maybe the ones on the wall." I was being facetious. The walls in here were hung with red silk curtains decorated with gold red stars. The awareness jolted me from my equilibrium.

Red and gold.

The room whirled around me rapidly. I was reminded of spinning globes and shooting gold glitter. Panicked, I had a momentary lapse of balance, and clutched at George in fright.

"What's up?" he asked alarmed.

I turned about, circling until I was dizzy, taking in the colours, the *intent* of the decor. This was a message to me. It had to be.

"The Mori. They've been under my nose this whole time."

Whittlecombe's General Stores were doing brisk business.

I was pleased to see Rhona and Stan busy in the shop. They were obviously working overtime with so many people visiting the village and the happy campers in the top field. People were queuing for all the essentials – milk, bacon, tea and toothpaste. And sweets.

I fell into the latter group. I plonked several bars of chocolate and two bottles of red wine on the counter. "And I'll have a bottle of your best brandy, please, Stan."

I dropped his name with accidental familiarly. He took a quick look at my face, but obviously didn't recognise me. Instead he smiled and politely totted up what I owed him. I caught Rhona giving me a sidelong glance in between the customers she was serving, and I thought I sensed a little animosity there. I wondered if it had anything to do with our reading.

I slunk back to George who was flicking through a car magazine by the newspaper stand at the front of the shop. I waited impatiently for him to decide whether he wanted to buy it or not.

At that moment a handsome young man with black curly hair walked in. Despite the coolness of the day he was wearing a pair of Bermuda shorts in pink, and matching flip flops, with a pristine white shirt and a filthy green apron. He carried a tray of aubergines from the vegetable display outside the shop.

"Could I take these, please," he asked, with a

thick accent, perhaps North African, and placed the aubergines on the counter.

"All of them?" asked Rhona, obviously taken aback.

"Yes please, madam. In fact, if you have any more, I can take them."

"I have plenty," Rhona sparkled.

"That's great news! I was relying on delivery to the Fayre, but my supplier has let me down at the last minute. I don't suppose you have more garlic too? I mean, lots of garlic."

"Strings?" Rhona confirmed, and the young man nodded. "Yes, I have plenty of strings of garlic too. What are you making?" she asked, and I listened in, curious to find out myself.

"Baba ghanoush. I'm having a complete run on it. The flat bread I make myself, and the baba ghanoush is just selling and selling. The campers love it!"

"You'll want lemons as well then," I called across the shop, full of enthusiasm.

Rhona shot me a look and narrowed her eyes. For one second I thought she'd seen through my Fenella disguise. I was reminded of the lemons conversation we had shared when we thought the whole village was coming down with flu the previous autumn.

I grabbed George's arm and pulled him out of the shop.

I couldn't shake the feeling that my disguise was beginning to slip.

George sipped at his wine while I nursed a brandy. Both of us were feeling a little flat after the day we'd had. Outside it was full dark now and the wind was getting up. We'd eaten our fill of baba ghanoush, flat bread, mixed salads and falafel and it had—as the young man in the General Stores promised—been delicious.

George sighed.

"What's up?" I asked, patting his knee.

"I don't feel like my undercover guise is working."

"No kidding?" I asked. He looked different to normal George for sure, but he didn't really carry off young and carefree as well as he imagined he did. "Well you need to mix it up a little. Possibly."

"How? What else can I do?" he drained his wine and reached for the bottle for a top-up. "Maybe I could get a job helping someone else out on one of their stalls. Do you know anyone who's looking for help?"

I shook my head and thought for a moment. Then it came to me. "Better than that, you could have your own stall."

"It's a bit late in the day for that," George said. "Besides what am I going to do? I don't know the first thing about tarot or telling fortunes, and I'm certainly no psychic."

"Not everyone at the Fayre is doing those things, are they?"

"No. That's true. Maybe I could open a coconut shy or something? Do you think Rhona has any coconuts?"

"Probably," I said. She had everything else.

"At least you don't have to be skilled to go around picking up coconuts after everyone."

"No," I said. "You don't. But there's already a coconut shy. I have another possibility. Something much easier on the back than bending down scooping up large hairy nuts all day long."

George's interest had been piqued. "Well?"

"You can sell things," I announced with a triumphant flourish of my arms.

George puffed his cheeks out, his face falling.

"Sell what? I don't have any stock, and it would be too complicated to source any now."

"Oh you give up far too easily." I could hear Gwyn's voice masquerading as my own. "Think about it. There's an empty booth right next door to mine now. This will give us an opportunity to shoot two birds with one stone." I lowered my voice and leaned in close to him. "Tomorrow you can go and find Lyle and ask him whether you can hire out the booth for the rest of the Fayre. Then you can ask him some questions about the previous tenant. See what we can find out about Kooky Kahlila."

George nodded. He could see the attraction of the idea. "But what am I going to sell?"

"Something peculiarly English, and terribly Whittlecombe." I paused for effect and reached for my mobile. "Tea and cake. I'm going to call the inn. We'll get Monsieur Emietter and Florence to bake you their best cakes, buns, scones and pastries. You'll sell out."

"It's nearly nine in the evening. They're hardly going to want to start baking now."

"They're ghosts, George," I said, listening to the burr as my mobile tried to connect to the inn. "Ghosts don't need sleep."

CHAPTER TEN

A t nine thirty the next morning, I escorted George into the lounge bar of The Hay Loft. Breakfast service was just finishing, so this seemed like an opportune time to grab the landlord. Lyle was perched on a stool on the punter's side of the bar, drinking coffee and reading a newspaper. I hung back and pretended to be engrossed in the specials board, allowing George the space to chat with Lyle.

"Excuse me," George started. "I was wondering if I could have a word?"

Lyle looked George up and down with vague disinterest. "Sure."

"Only I couldn't help but notice that there's a booth at the Fayre that's empty."

"Right?"

"And I'd like to hire it for the next few days—if

153

the person that originally had it, isn't coming back that is."

"Which booth is it?"

"Number 46. On the right-hand side of the field."

Lyle stood and walked around to the other side of the bar, rummaged under the counter and then produced a copy of the ground plan for the Fayre. He spread it out on top of the bar. "Number 46," he murmured, running a stubby finger along the crumpled paper. "Forty-six. Oh yeah. Yeah. Right." He flipped the plan around so that George could see it. "This one?" he asked, "In between Fabulous Fenella and Dan the Spookman?"

Dan the Spookman? Why hadn't I noticed him before? I looked over my shoulder at Lyle and George, itching to step up closer and take a better look at the map.

"That's it?"

"Mmm. Kooky Kahlila..." Lyle frowned. "I think... I don't know to be honest..."

I could see George had his best innocent face on, although given his rough disguise, innocent didn't really cut the mustard.

Lyle grunted. "Look. Just give me a minute will you? I need to make a phone call."

"Of course." George bowed graciously, taking a step away from the bar and looking elsewhere in a very polite and peculiarly self-deprecating British manner. Of course he could still hear every word Lyle said. We both could. Lyle wasn't one to use a hushed tone when his bellow would do.

"Hey," Lyle said into the receiver. "It's Lyle. Yeah. Yep. Listen. Kooky Kahlila? What's the deal there? I mean what's happened to her?" He listened, then, "Really? Right. Yeah. So she's not coming back? And you don't need the booth? You sure?"

The hairs on the back of my neck prickled. Who exactly was Lyle chatting to? Somebody he was in cahoots with, that seemed certain from the way he was talking. There was a power relationship evident here, some kind of hierarchy, and Lyle was calling *up* the food chain not *down* it.

"Will do. Cheers bye."

He put the phone down and caught George's attention. "Yeah, you're good to go, mate. I'll need you to fill in a form, and then it's all yours." George moved back to the bar and I came to stand with him. Thankfully, Lyle ignored me.

He plucked a clipboard from the wall, laying it on the counter in front of us, freed a batch of forms from the top, leaving everything underneath dishevelled. He handed the forms to George, but I was more interested in what had been left behind. It was upside down. I needed a clearer look.

George rummaged in his own pocket for a pen. I trod on his toe heavily, stilling him. "You wouldn't have a pen, would you?" I asked the landlord sweetly.

Lyle nodded and disappeared into his office. I quickly swivelled the clipboard around to look at the single sheet of headed notepaper wedged under the clip.

Curly writing, reminiscent of Victorian engraving. Just one word.

Astutus.

I ripped the sheet free and quickly stuffed it into my pocket.

At last we had another definite link between Lyle Cavendish and Astutus.

Whether that translated to evidence that Astutus were a front for The Mori, well that remained to be seen.

I stared at the tarot card on the floor of Kahlila's booth.

Unable to bear the red and gold décor, I'd decided to rip the wallcoverings down, leaving George to unpack the goods. We'd shipped a load of crockery to the Fayre from the inn via taxi, borrowed a couple of patio sets and covered the tables in check tablecloths, so that people could sit and have a break while they wandered round the Fayre if they wished.

While I gathered up the material to chuck into a black bin bag, a tarot card fell to the floor. The image landed facing me, the right way up. The High Priestess.

Nothing is as it seems.

I scooped the card up and flipped it over. Old and well-used, the reverse side matched the one poor Mr Bramble had been clutching.

Was there an additional meaning to this card? Taken out of context it was difficult to know.

George called me outside. I hurriedly stuffed the card down the front of my robe and joined him, to help finish setting up.

Florence and Monsieur Emietter had done us proud. There were enormous fluffy scones—plain, fruit and cheese. They arrived accompanied by a huge tub of clotted cream and Florence's homemade jam, several large and luscious sponge cakes, mini quiches, Millionaires shortbread, chocolate rice crispy squares, and some very interesting Devon violet muffins.

Needless to say, George's tea and cake stall was a resounding success.

As I'd known he would, he soon found his rhythm and enjoyed being able to chat to the customers as he served them. I hoped he'd garner plenty of intel for his undercover mission.

In the meantime, for Fenella, it was back to fortune telling. I carried on where I'd left off the previous day, covering the orb in black velvet material, talking to the client, waving my hands over the cloth and then revealing the orb. All good fun.

When I could, I hung out with George, listening in on conversations, and surreptitiously watching the other stallholders, particularly keen to get a glimpse of the mysterious Dan the Spookman if he ever surfaced.

But he never did. His booth remained closed.

All the time, my mind kept returning to the tarot card I'd found. I'd never suspected Kooky Kahlila of working with The Mori for a minute, in spite of finding her trying to snoop around my booth. I'd assumed that for the most part the people participating in the Fayre were genuine *people*, even if they were genuine *fakes*. There were one or two that I could tell were all about the showmanship and had never spoken to the spirit world in their lives. They were great actors and skilled amateur psychologists, adept at pulling the wool over people's eyes, and while I applauded anyone for making a living, I worried about those customers who were vulnerable to anyone peddling complete bunkum.

And for my part, Fenella tried hard to present what she saw truthfully, and offered only positive interpretations, and hope for the future.

By 4.30 pm, George was completely out of cake. I'd eaten my share and had a sugar overdose. Having tea on tap in the booth next door, had also meant rather more intermissions to the lavatory than usual. I'd spotted the queues for Mama Henri's shows, and that had reminded me that I really wanted to get in and watch her perform at some stage.

I shut up shop for the day, and helped George tidy his booth, then we headed back to my caravan to have a rest. When I suggested catching Mama Henri's performance he agreed, and just after six we headed back out into the evening to join the queue.

Josiah sold us tickets, again staring at me most queerly, and we took seats on benches in the second row. The marquee filled up with spectators, with some standing at the back. The lights were dimmed, and smoke rolled across the little stage, and then the sound of tribal drums erupted around the auditorium.

Mama Henri shimmied out of the wings and onto the stage, draped in a large snake, and a few strategically placed clothes. I coin that word loosely. She appeared to be wearing nothing more than small squares of chamois leather on bits of string. She performed an energetic dance with the snake, her moves powerful and earthy, her skin shining under the lights.

After a few brief words with the audience, she took us through how she conjured spirits. The lighting was used to good effect, dipping the auditorium—such as it was—into darkness to ramp up the tension. She would talk to us, her voice low and intimate so that we had to strain to hear what she was saying, and then from nowhere loud drums would break into the silence and we'd all jump out of our skins.

Smoke, from a floor level smoke machine, rolled around our ankles, rising slowly. Again, using the lights, it was relatively easy for her to trick us into believing that the spirits of our ancestors were following us around the Fayre.

I did look around, but neither Gwyn, nor my father, were anywhere to be seen.

In between times, Mama Henri described certain spells we could use against enemies, or to attract a partner. I had a lot of fun and had to admit she had a great sales technique.

"What did you make of that?" I asked George, linking my arm through his as we exited the marquee into the chill of the night.

"Dramatic," he said, widening his eyes. "Blimey. A bit scary."

I giggled. "You great softy." Most of it had been smoke and mirrors. Perhaps projections. I had no doubt at all that Mama Henri was the real deal, but she also gave good theatre.

George and I made our way down the path. They Fayre had quietened down now. Most of the other stallholders had finished for the evening, with the exception of a few sideshows, and of course the fun fair in full swing in the next field. Jolly music drifted to us from that way, people screaming and shouting as they spun and tumbled on the faster rides. The Big Wheel, with its hundreds of brightly coloured rainbow bulbs, lit up the sky above Whittle-combe. Such a cheerful sight.

"What do you fancy for supper?" George asked, fishing out his wallet.

"Well it's been twenty-four hours since my last sausage fix, so I vote for Parker's Porky Perfection."

"Parker's what?"

"Have you not indulged in the delight that is a Parker Banger yet?"

George shook his head. "Obviously not."

I dragged him down the path from Mama Henri's marquee, until he could see where Rob's green and gold liveried van with its open sides had been parked. There was a small queue. We joined it and George began reading the menu of sausages with obvious delight.

"Now you're talking," he said. "Why eat baba ghanoush when you can stuff yourself with sausages?"

Rob smiled to see me standing on the other side of his counter. "Well if it isn't Fabulous Fenella again. Always a treat."

"It is for me certainly, and this time I've brought my friend along," I told Rob. "He's always hungry, and by the sound of it he likes sausages too."

"Oh I do," George nodded with enthusiasm. "I do."

"Good news. What can I get you both?"

I opted for plain pork sausage, mash and gravy and George chose sausages with cider, chips, peas and gravy. As I said, he's always hungry.

Rob set to grilling the sausages and served a couple of hot drinks to a few people waiting behind us, then when they had left, he returned to where I was waiting and leaned over the counter. Lowering his voice he asked, "You remember what we were talking about the other day?"

I cast a glance at George and he narrowed his eyes and stepped closer, so he could hear Rob too.

"Yes."

"Well, I've been keeping an eye out and now I do have something to report. Something weird."

"Go on," I said.

Rob looked around nervously. "It could be something and nothing."

George shook his head. "Some of the best information is shared that way."

"Okay." Rob breathed out nervously. "You know, depending on how busy I am, I keep the van open as late as possible. Maximise my potential you know? It's going to be another six weeks or so before I start doing regular daily summer events, so I need to make the best of this for now. It being on the doorstep and all that."

"Yes." I nodded impatiently, waiting for him to get to the crux.

"So, last night I was serving till just after half past nine, I had people coming over from the fair, you know? Then it takes me a good hour to clean the van thoroughly. All the grease and fat gets everywhere so you need to knuckle down and get on with it."

George and I nodded, and Rob hesitated. "I start with the cooker, the hob, the hood, that sort of thing and then finish with the counters and the hatches. But last night, I had an issue with one of the refrigerators and it took me ages to fix the problem and clear up the mess, so I didn't close the hatches till closer to midnight. It was while I was cleaning the hatch that I spotted something out of the ordinary."

"What?" I whispered.

"People?" George asked.

Rob shook his head. "No, and this is where it's going to sound daft." He laughed nervously and glanced around again.

I did the same. You never really knew who was watching or listening. It was hard to tell in the semi-darkness, with so much shadow around. Many of the booths were in complete darkness so the only light came from the food trucks and stalls that were still open. Generators buzzed in the distance. People sauntered here and there, talking, laughing, eating and drinking.

"Go on," George urged him.

"Lights." Rob said. "Strange lights."

"Like UFOs?" George's voice remained level, but I sensed an air of weary resignation emanating from him.

But I knew exactly what Rob was going to say.

"No. At least I don't think so. These were small. Quite low to the ground."

I didn't want to prompt him, so I held my tongue.

"How low?" asked George.

"Difficult to say because they were up the field a bit. Not high in the sky, not on the ground."

"What did they look like?" George asked.

"Like balls. I had the sense that they were the size of a football or something. Not massive by any means. I probably wouldn't have noticed them at all, except—"

"Except?"

"They were a bright red. Like a pillar box red. They stood out because of all the gold. The lights that were on outside Mama Henri's marquee meant I could see them. It was the gold that caught my eye. This sparkling colour."

My stomach rolled uncomfortably. The Mori.

"Like a Christmas bauble," Rob finished.

George glanced at me. I knew what he was thinking. I'd described to him on several occasions the shimmering red globes, and he knew of The Mori, although he had never found any actual evidence of their existence.

I found my voice. "Could you see what they were doing?"

Rob looked up the field as though looking for them. "They floated around the stalls and booths, hanging in the air like balloons, but spinning. Then they all came together."

George frowned. "How many are we talking?"

"Mmm," Rob thought for a second. "Maybe eight or so."

Eight of The Mori in one place? That wasn't something to take lightly. I would have to let Wizard Shadowmender know about this.

"They came together," I pressed. "Then what happened."

"They hung together as thought they were having a conflab. Ridiculous as it might seem. Then they started drifting down this way, heading for the gate. At that stage I was a little spooked, I must admit. I ducked down behind the counter here and waited for them to pass me."

Rob laughed nervously. "Bonkers, I know."

"Not at all," I said with feeling. "Better to be safe than sorry. You did the right thing."

"Does that mean anything to you?" Rob asked and started flipping sausages and stirring his gravy.

"It certainly does," I said. "I'm just not sure what yet."

"By gum, they were delicious," George said, finishing off his dinner. He sat across from me, mopping up the gravy with some bread. I'd hardly touched mine. I pushed my plate over to him.

"You can finish these off if you want," I offered.

George frowned. "What's up?"

"Fenella is watching her weight," I joked.

George speared one of my sausages. "Are you bothered by what Rob told us?"

"Of course I am. Aren't you?" I asked pointedly. "Perhaps you don't believe me when I tell you that The Mori are a real threat. Not just to me and the inn, but to ordinary people in and around Whittlecombe and probably much further afield."

George chewed and looked at me, an expression I couldn't read on his face.

"I'm not making it up, you know. I saw them that night in Speckled Wood. There were dozens of them. And then I found one in Derek Pearce's bedroom. Something is going on and we don't have a grip on what it is."

George sighed. I hoped he didn't think I was being hysterical.

I folded my arms and glared at him. "If you're thinking that I'm the only one who's seen evidence of them then you're wrong. Rob has too. I didn't set that up. You heard what he said."

George held his hands up in mock surrender. "I do believe you, Alf," he said. I widened my eyes to warn him about using my name and put my fingers to my lips. We were being too loud.

He lowered his voice. "But at the moment, I'm not sure what it is you think The Mori want, or even what we can do about it."

I began to protest, and he carried on, "You're probably right that they were involved in the death of Derek Pearce. I've found no other leads on that case. Not even the traces of chemicals we discovered that had been stored in the shed on Derek's allotment helped us out. Remember them? We haven't been able to discover where those chemicals ended up or what Derek might have used them for. In fact, even now, we don't know what the chemicals would be used for at all. Do you have any ideas on that score?"

I shook my head. I didn't have any clue what The Mori were planning. I couldn't help but feel sore that George didn't share my sense of urgency or dread about The Mori. Quite clearly, because he hadn't seen them with his own eyes, he found it difficult to take me seriously.

We lapsed into a cold silence.

George collected up the dishes. "I'll wash these up," he said, an element of bewilderment in his tone. Were we arguing? I hated to think we were. We never had before. He avoided looking at me, simply placed all the dirty crockery and cutlery into the washing up bowl and stepped out of the caravan, heading for the washing up and rubbish disposal area that had been set up at the bottom of the field.

Left alone, I lay back on the seat and sighed. Then I remembered the letter I'd brought back from the inn the other night. I reached into my bag and drew it out, turning it over and over in my hands, looking for clues as to who had sent it, but there was nothing to distinguish it from a million other letters in white envelopes sent on any given day. The typography of the printed envelope was anonymous. There were no marks apart from the Exeter post mark.

I slit the envelope open with my thumb nail and reluctantly drew the contents out. A single sheet of A4. The letters had been carefully cut out using the same pamphlet for the Fayre as the last few letters had, by now I recognised the colours.

Tick tock

The clocks spring forward in two days.

Are you ready to meet your winter?

It was my birthday in two days. I hadn't forgotten, I just didn't know how I could celebrate something that was uniquely about me as Alf, when I looked and felt more like Fenella.

The words were ominous and yet oddly surreal. I crumpled the letter in my hand as I heard George clumping up the steps of the caravan. He dropped the plastic bowl on the floor, the contents still filthy, and beckoned to me, holding a finger to his lips.

"What—?" I started to ask him, but he gave me a warning glance and reached out to take my hand and guide me down the steps. I dropped the crumpled paper ball on the floor and followed George outside.

There was no moon to speak of—perhaps the cloud was low—and the camp site was dark. Some tents were lit inside by torches or other lights, casting strange shadows against the plastic or canvas walls. Elsewhere, solar lights helped us avoid guy ropes, but otherwise there was very little light to navigate by. The evening was cool, almost cold, and my breath came in steamy little gasps.

I held onto George as he led me down towards the wash station, but before we got there he detoured slightly and stopped. "I waited here because both the sinks were taken, and I wanted to watch what was going on around the camp for a bit," he whispered, his voice so quiet I could barely hear him. "And do you know what I saw?"

I looked around, to see whether it was obvious. "No," I whispered back, and he pointed out over the hedge into the next field. I followed his finger. The field next to the campsite was empty. One of the local farmers grazed cows here, but they were being kept elsewhere for the duration of the Fayre. At first I couldn't see anything at all, but gradually as my eyes became more accustomed to the darkness, I thought I spotted something moving. Small shapes.

"Foxes maybe?" I whispered to George. That wouldn't be unusual. "Or badgers?"

"Wait."

We stood stock still, George hardly breathing. I

could sense some tension in him and wondered at that, and then I saw what he meant, and my breath caught audibly in my throat. Red lights. Too far away to make much else out, but undeniably red and certainly not the glowing of animal eyes in the darkness. I counted the lights I could see. Five.

"What are they doing?" I whispered.

"When I first noticed them, it was because one shot across the field on the other side of the hedge," George said. "Rob was right. It was about the size of a football, with a gold shimmer."

"Now they're just hanging around in a cold field."

"Weird."

"Where are the rest of them?" I asked, turning slowly about and peering among the tents and caravans dotted around the field. "Rob said there were more than this."

"He said eight, didn't he?" George took my arm. "Let's have a look around, shall we?"

We skirted the hedge, following it around to the bottom of the field, but there was no way of getting closer to the lights, and we couldn't gain access. Instead we turned about and retraced our steps until we were able to pass through the gate to the Fayre's field. We sneaked behind the booths there, unoccupied at this time of night, and shrouded in darkness, and walked around behind several food trucks. One or two of these still had lights on inside and a couple had people hovering around, just chilling out and smoking or drinking, but not really interested in us.

The hedges, standing on embankments here, were too high to look over, and too wide and thick to peer through. But at last, behind Mama Henri's marquee, we spotted a stile, virtually invisible among the wild undergrowth. George climbed onto the wooden spur and stared across into the field before jumping back down beside me. "Rats. They've gone."

"We've lost them then?"

"Let's look around the Fayre. Rob said he saw them moving through the field."

We made our way back into the main drag, now devoid of people, the tents and booths silent and dark. I glanced down the path towards Rob's van, thinking we were standing approximately where he had first seen the lights, and something new caught my eye. A glow.

Not red but orange.

"George?" Reaching back for him I tugged his coat. I took a few steps, trying to get him to follow me. "What is that?" I asked, dropping my grip and moving more quickly.

"What's up?" George asked.

"Rob's van." I started to run, hindered by my long robes.

"It's on fire," George shouted and pelted past me. "Fire!" he yelled, trying to alert others to the situation. I ran after him, but he waved me off. "Stay back!" he ordered, but I ignored him.

He dashed round to the rear of the van, with me on his heels. The door had been wedged shut with the long arm of a broom tucked under the handle.

"What on earth?" I asked. Why would someone have wedged the door closed unless...?

"Is Rob still in there?" My shriek rent through the night.

"Call the fire service, Alf!" George yanked the wooden shaft of the broom away, then ripped his jacket off, winding it around his fist to wear as a glove so that he could clasp the steel door handle without burning himself. "Now stand back!"

He flung the door wide open and I had a glimpse of fiery hell inside the van. Rob lay on the floor as the fire raged at head height. George ducked inside, crouched and inched forwards on his hands and knees to where Rob was lying, and in seconds had gripped the other man under the arms and was pulling him across the floor of the van. Once he had Rob's head out of the door, I helped to drag him down onto the grass. Together we half-dragged and half-carried the unconscious sausage supremo away from the van.

I didn't have my mobile on me, but fortunately other people had been alerted by George's call for assistance and someone had already placed a call. It was far too late for the van though. It burned like a torch, lighting up the whole field.

I leaned over Rob as George checked for a pulse. I could see he had taken a nasty knock to the head. The stench of smoke clung to him but there appeared to be no obvious sign of injury. As we watched over him, me clutching his hand, George gently slapping the side of his cheek and asking Rob whether he could hear him, Rob's eyes fluttered open. He looked confused, but at least he was conscious.

"What happened?" he asked, his voice thick through smoke inhalation, his eyes red rimmed.

"We could ask you the same thing," I said. "You frightened us to death."

"Someone knocked on the door," he said.

"Who was it? Did you get a look at their face?" George asked.

Rob coughed, and waved a hand in front of himself. "I saw red. I just saw red ... and then bam! I don't remember anything else."

I stared grimly at George. He pursed his lips and nodded.

"You could have been killed," I said to Rob, my voice shaking.

"My van," he cried, and struggled to sit up.

"Easy there, buddy." George restrained him. "It's too late for the van now. But at least you're safe."

Thank goodness, I thought.

The Mori had not claimed another victim tonight, although it had been a close-run thing.

I insisted George spend the night in the caravan with me. I couldn't settle. My clothes and hair stank of smoke and I desperately wanted a shower, but it was late, and the night was cold. I couldn't face the unisex cubicles. I'd have to wait till morning.

We tuned the radio to a classic station and let the gentle music help to unwind us. I nursed a brandy, and George drank beer straight from the bottle. We kept our voices low, huddled together in the subdued light of one lamp.

"Is it a coincidence that Rob told us about the red lights and was then attacked and his van destroyed?" I asked. Beside me George shook his head.

"No, I don't think so. I mean it could be. We have no evidence—"

"With you it's always about evidence," I said mournfully, frustrated he couldn't see things the way I did.

"That's the nature of my job, you know it is—"

I did know that but nonetheless it irritated me. "I sense it," I said. "I sense *them*. They're around us, and I feel like they are closing in."

George took a swig of his beer. "Maybe they never really went anywhere."

I considered what he'd said. Remembered the early days after The Battle for Speckled Wood. "You might be right. I thought they'd gone. But I'd certainly started to sense their presence again by October. And now..."

"They're becoming bolder?"

"Yes."

George shifted his weight. "Perhaps they're afraid of someone or something."

"What could that be?" I took another sip of my

brandy. It was doing the business, warming me through, smoothing off the edges, blunting the memory of the hot fierce flames just a foot or so above poor Rob's head. If we had seen the fire seconds later, or been distracted by something else...

It really didn't bear thinking about.

CHAPTER ELEVEN

Sleep eluded me for the most part and when I dragged my sorry self down to the shower block next morning, I spent longer than normal under the tepid water. Partly I needed the cascade to wake me up, and partly I wanted to ensure the acrid stench of burning had been rinsed properly away from my hair and every pore in my skin. The water pummelled my face as I attempted to empty my mind of thoughts of The Mori.

It must be a tiny bit like having post-traumatic stress disorder. A flash of red at any time could cause a surge of panic to rush through my body. It would stop me breathing, leave my heart racing, while I glanced around wide-eyed. Invariably all I'd see would be a woman or a child in a red jacket or sweater. Occasionally it was a letter box or telephone kiosk. At such times I had to give myself a little shake and re-centre myself.

The atmosphere at The Fayre had changed subtly. Obviously the campers—particularly those who had been on scene the previous evening—were aware of all the drama that had occurred. They began the day by inspecting the skeletal wreckage of Rob's van from a safe distance or standing around in small groups chatting about what had happened or what they had seen.

George and I, on the scrounge for illicit intelligence, drifted among these clumps of bystanders, listening to what they had to say. It seemed nobody had actually seen anything of note. I realised many of them were simply bigging up their parts in the drama to make themselves sound more grandiose and important. Absolutely nobody offered us anything new.

But others—the genuine psychics and tellers— that was a different story. I saw haunted looks on some faces and sensed a deep feeling of unease. For them at least, there was an understanding that something unnatural had occurred the previous night. While the common-sense explanation suggested the culprits were kids messing around, unintentional arson perhaps, others knew that something untoward and supernatural had walked among us.

While George unpacked his morning delivery of cakes, biscuits, scones and pastries, freshly arrived from Whittle Inn, I opened my booth and prepared for my first reading. Dusting the orb I settled it in the centre of the table. It sparkled as I did so, and I gazed into it with curiosity. Generally it never spoke only to me, and yet here it sat, buzzing with energy and demanding my attention.

I closed the stabled door and slipped the latch across so I couldn't be disturbed. Then I pulled up a chair and drew the orb to me, peering deeply into the white clouds there. They bubbled and popped, then cleared, and Wizard Shadowmender's head appeared, his cheeks a cheerful red as though he'd been sitting too close to the fire.

"Good morning, Alf!" he boomed at me.

"Morning," I said, and smiled to see him.

"I understand you had a bit of a commotion on site last night?"

How had he found that out? Millicent maybe. I knew she often updated him about the happenings around Whittlecombe. "Yes," I said. "A food van was set alight."

"Our friends?"

"Almost definitely. George and I both saw the spinning globes in a neighbouring field. And then when we rescued Rob—the owner of the van—from the inferno, he said something about 'seeing red' and he definitely didn't mean he was angry."

The wizard nodded. "Why would they target him?"

That was the terrible thing, wasn't it? I twisted my face in misery. "He mentioned the existence of the red lights to me. He'd been looking out for anything unusual because I told him I'd had a break-in here at my booth." I sighed. "Basically I lied. I feel terrible about it."

The old wizard nodded and stroked his beard. "Have you been able to uncover much information?"

"Not really. I had a woman in the booth next to me. She went by the name of Kooky Kahlila, but she disappeared a few days ago. Then George and I spoke to Lyle and heard him make a phone call to someone. They definitely knew who Kahlila was and that she'd done her job—whatever that might have been. I'm not sure how that helps us." I remembered the clipboard. "But I did see some headed notepaper Lyle was using. I stole a sheet of it. It was Astutus for sure."

I pondered over the past few days. "Other than

that I'm not sure I've gotten anything useful. I met a strange woman called Mama Henri—she's a voodoo priestess with an entrancing show—and she came to visit me and offer her help. It was all a bit mysterious. Then last night we saw the lights."

"How many did you see?"

"I only saw five or six last night, but Rob the sausage seller claimed to have seen more the previous evening."

"Is that so?" Wizard Shadowmender sighed. "Alf, listen to me carefully." His face was deadly serious, his eyes troubled. "We've had some intel that suggests that dark factions of warlocks are gathering together. It may be something and it may be nothing. They may not be anywhere near Whittlecombe, but given what you've seen, I'm inclined to pull you out now."

"Pull me out?"

"Send you back to your inn, as yourself. You're safer there. You don't have any protection at the Fayre."

"I have George." It was a half-hearted interjection.

"He's a lovely man." We both knew that in the face of what The Mori were capable of, George could only ever be an observer. "But, I'd prefer you to be at home, where the circle of protection we have around the grounds will keep you safe."

I frowned. I didn't want to leave just yet. I wanted to find out more about The Mori. "Wizard Shadowmender, the Fayre ends tomorrow evening and I'll have to go home then at any rate. Given what George and I witnessed last night, I'd really like to stick around and see if they make a repeat appearance tonight."

"Go home," Wizard Shadowmender repeated. "Take a good hot bubble bath with your Cosmetic Blaster Caster and embrace the real you."

I sighed. I couldn't disobey. "That will certainly be a relief after nearly a week of being Fenella," I said and Shadowmender laughed.

"Also while I'm thinking of it, I am going to adjust the orb so that it is a two-way telecaster. You can use it to get in touch with me. This will make it easier if you ever have an emergency and the orb is to hand. Saves on those new-fangled telephones and things. I really can't get to grips with them."

"Okay," I said, hiding a smirk. "Thanks."

"And I'm going to arrange for Finbarr to come down to the inn to be with you for a few days while we try and take stock of everything that seems to be going on in the world. It's better to be safe than sorry."

"I suppose so," I said, sure he could sense my reluctance. I couldn't help but feel disappointed. What had I achieved here at the Fayre?

"Take that look off your face," Wizard Shadowmender smiled good-naturedly. "I'll arrange for the caravan and the booth to be taken away, and for Neptune to be collected from the stables. All Fenella needs to do is disappear. So go home."

Except it wasn't that easy.

As soon as I unlatched the stable door, I found several clients outside waiting for a reading, and that kept me busy for the next few hours. I finally surfaced at midday, intent on grabbing some lunch. George was as busy as he had been the day before. I helped him out for a while, slicing cakes, plating cream teas, pouring tea. The kettle boiled endlessly and the chore of clearing plates and rubbish from the little patio sets seemed to never end.

Finally, we managed a breather.

"Wizard Shadowmender wants me to call it quits," I informed George, as he washed another bowl full of crockery and I waited for the tea to brew in one of Florence's largest teapots.

"And finish up at the Fayre?"

"Yes." I pouted. "I don't feel like I'm any closer to knowing anything important that can help us."

George gave me a pointed look. "Given what happened last night, I'm not sure quitting is such a bad idea."

"Has there been any word on Rob?" I asked. George had been in a better position to overhear the latest gossip all morning, while I'd been tied up in my booth.

He nodded, looking somewhat relieved. "Yes. The word is he was released from hospital this morning. Some smoke inhalation and a concussion, but nothing life threatening. He's going to sort out the insurance as soon as he's feeling up to it."

"Oh, that is good news. That was a nice new van he had."

"He lives in one of your cottages, doesn't he?"

"Yes, Sparrow Cottage."

"We'll have to pop in and see how he's doing."

"Take him a cake," I grinned.

George finished drying and stacking the plates, ready to re-use.

"Maybe birthday cake," he teased.

Birthday cake.

Tomorrow was my birthday. And the first day of spring.

I recalled the letters in the file in the drawer in my office and shivered.

'When spring begins, you will meet your winter.'

Perhaps heading back to Whittle Inn wouldn't be such a bad idea.

A customer at the booth drew my attention, and I decided that I'd wind the afternoon up with a final batch of curious customers, then go and pack my belongings in the caravan before heading back to the inn.

I finished up with my first visitor of the afternoon, fully expecting there to be a queue outside when I showed her out, but nobody was waiting. Checking to my right I could see that even George was less busy than he'd been. The brownie stall had also closed.

I edged out into what had until recently been a busy thoroughfare, and quickly realised that a fair few of the stalls and sideshows were already closed, and others were preparing to do so. Mama Henri's marquee which dominated the rear of the field, was in the process of being dismantled.

People were heading home already.

I frowned. Turning about, I wondered if I'd missed something. Morton, the mountain rune reader was strolling purposefully down the mud path towards me, hauling a small cart with his tent and all his belongings.

"Fabulous Alfanella," he called, drawing up alongside me.

"Are you going home?" I asked.

"Yes. Back to Bremanger."

"I'm sorry to hear that," I said. "We didn't really get a chance to hang out."

"You'll have to visit me in Norway."

I smiled. "I'd like that. And if you're ever back this way, please come and stay at Whittle Inn. Although if you do, you'll have to mind your head on the ceilings. Some of them are very low."

He laughed and reached out to shake my hand. "Why are you going today?" I asked.

Morton shrugged his huge wide shoulders. "Everything has changed today. Do you not feel it? There's something in the air. Something disturbing. Yesterday Whittlecombe seemed such a lovely, friendly place, full of people eager to learn and share. Today, it is not a good place to be."

"Because of the fire?" I asked, nodding in the direction of Rob's ruined van.

"Who knows. Something heavy has settled here. I choose not to stay."

He regarded me seriously. "You know," he said, his voice lowering with sincerity. "I think you should pay heed to the runes. I worry for you."

"I am taking it seriously," I reassured him. "I'm planning on heading home myself now."

"That's good. Take care."

I shook his hand and bade him a good journey, watching him trundle down the path to the exit close to The Hay Loft. The sky, so clear this morning had taken on a darker grey cast. Black clouds to the west of us appeared ominous. At some stage we were going to have a downpour. That would only encourage even more campers to leave. Who wants to try and live in a muddy field?

"Excuse me?"

I turned to see a young woman with a small child in a pushchair. "Hi."

"Would it be possible to get a reading or are you closed as well? I've tried a few places, but they've all started packing up, or they are booked out for the afternoon." She peered around me, looking into the booth. My table was still set up, the orb on its stand.

I couldn't disappoint her. I'd go as soon as I'd wrapped up the reading with her.

"Of course," I said, and showed her in.

In fact, I remained busy for the rest of the afternoon, and so couldn't take the opportunity to get away early. At around four I recognised the sound of fat raindrops hitting the felt roof above my head. By the time I'd shown my final client of the afternoon out an hour and a half later, the low sky was heavy with thick black cloud and the rain fell relentlessly.

George had obviously given up for the day. Who could blame him? Florence's wonderful cakes must have ended up a soggy mess. I skipped next door and peered into the window. His booth had been cleared and everything tidied neatly away. I wondered where he'd gone.

Turning back to my own booth for the final time, intent on stowing the orb safely away, I discovered an envelope tacked to the top half of the stable door. I plucked it off, imagining it must be some missive from Lyle or The Hay Loft about money owed, an invoice maybe, or perhaps even a message from George.

My name on the envelope had been printed not handwritten, but it was addressed to Alfhild Daemonne. Only George and the folk at the Whittle Inn should know I was Alf and not Fabulous Fenella.

Wasn't that right?

I ripped the envelope open and pulled out the card from inside. A cute owl holding a birthday cake.

Happy birthday.

That seemed innocent enough. So why were my hands shaking? I flipped the cover open. A tarot card fell out. Inside, a short lyrical message. To the point.

'*The end is nigh. Tonight you die.*'

Absolutely nothing else to see. No clue as to the sender.

I bent down to retrieve the tarot card. I already knew it would be another one from Kooky Kahlila's deck. I pondered the image as I looked at it on the floor, reversed. The Emperor. Masculine, greedy, manipulative, sometimes symbolising power and control.

Shadowmender had been right. My cover had been blown at the Fayre and now there was nothing for it but for me to get back to my wonky inn and hunker down until reinforcements arrived. Some important game was being played out here in Whittlecombe. As far as I could see this wasn't about me specifically, but I was becoming embroiled in something far bigger than I could handle.

I hurried back to the caravan. The number of tents on the camp site had diminished by at least half. George's tent was still in place, surviving under the onslaught of all the water falling out of the sky in stair rods, although looking a little sorry for itself to be sure.

I rummaged through the drawers and cupboards, collecting my bits and pieces together, ensuring I had everything I had brought with me, and everything I needed. Once Wizard Shadowmender took the caravan back, I guessed it would be impossible to retrieve anything I'd left behind. Most of my belongings would fit comfortably into one rucksack. The caravan had been so well kitted out I'd hardly brought anything of my own.

I decided to leave a couple of notes for George. I didn't want him to worry about my disappearance. I plonked myself down on my bunk to pen a couple of messages, one to leave here in the caravan in plain sight, and the other one I intended to take to his tent and leave attached to his sleeping bag. Then I pondered whether to phone Charity and let her know I was heading home. It wasn't so much that I wanted the inn to roll out the red carpet—although that might have been nice—but just so she knew to expect me and perhaps they could save me some dinner. It would be nice to have something home cooked after so long surviving on take-away food, as nice as some of it had undoubtedly been.

I elected not to phone, and instead, with one last look at the caravan, my note to George on the small fold down table, I stepped out into the evening rain.

There were five steps down to the ground, but as my foot reached for the bottom step, it seemed to disappear beneath me. I slipped, falling backwards, expecting to land on the steps, but instead someone caught me and held me firmly, and the rucksack was yanked away from my grasp. I opened my mouth to scream and instantly found it covered by a cloth. I smelt something strange, oddly metallic, and lashed out in a frenzy, unable to see who was doing this. There must have been a second person because someone caught my hands and restricted my movement.

Then I knew no more.

CHAPTER TWELVE

For some time I drifted in and out of consciousness. Awaking the first time, my stomach churned with nausea. All was dark and still. I could hear the faint sounds of the Fayre, what was left of it, still happening around me. People talking and laughing, music from the sideshows and rides. The bass made my head thump and I retched. I closed my eyes and lapsed into semi-unconsciousness, grateful for the darkness.

The second time I awoke, the nausea had eased. While I'd been out of it someone had moved me into the back of a vehicle. I'd rolled myself into a ball, and felt disoriented, but even so, I felt the bustle and jostle of movement, the vibration from the engine, and heard the bass thrum that told me I had to be in a car or a van. I shifted position, and tried to loft my head up, but I still couldn't see anything. A hood or a mask covered my face, and my hands had been bound behind me. I waited for a hot rush of panic to claw at my insides, but my fuzzy head couldn't compute what was happening or work out how much danger I might be in.

We had to be travelling along winding lanes, that much I understood from the way the vehicle moved, and the occasions it slowed down, presumably to let something pass. As the ride became bumpier, I knew we were heading off the beaten track. The harsh jerks and rough bouncing caused my nausea to return. I closed my eyes and gratefully slipped away.

On the final occasion I came to, I shivered with cold. While I still couldn't see, I sensed night must have fallen. I lay on a cold, hard floor—concrete or possibly stone. At first I thought everything was quiet and still, until somewhere I heard water dripping, and the scamper of tiny animals close by.

My left arm had gone to sleep because of the position I found myself in, and I groaned and tried to straighten out. It was difficult. My feet had been bound too and my back had been placed against a hard surface. Now was the time for panic, I could only imagine I'd been buried alive. I cried out and thrashed around as best as I was able, hitting my head painfully against the floor as I did so.

"Easy," came a distorted male voice in the darkness. Not one I recognised.

I lay still, panting under my face covering. "Who is that?" I asked. "Can you help me."

"You were given fair warning, Alfhild." A second voice. Cultured. An older gentleman perhaps. "We asked you to step away from our affairs, but you had to carry on meddling."

I froze. The owner of this voice had to be the person who'd been sending me the death threats. The Mori?

"I'm sorry it's come to this. I really am." The voice didn't sound remotely regretful.

My heart beat so loudly in my chest I was sure he could hear it. I tried to quell my rising dismay and keep a careful lid on my panic. If I could stay in control... perhaps I could get out of this situation.

Maybe I could reason with the voice. "Please let me go," I tried. "I haven't seen your face. I won't say anything. I'll just go back to my inn and mind my own business."

The man laughed, a humourless chuckle. "That seems unlikely given your past form."

"I'll pack my bags. Close the inn." *Over my dead body*.

"You would never do that, Alfhild. And besides, it's too late for that now. We're committed."

Whom did he mean by we? "Committed to what? What are you going to do with me?"

"Oh I'd hate to ruin your birthday surprise," the voice said, and it rang with amusement. "So I suggest you just sit tight and wait to see how our little celebratory party pans out. Just be patient. It won't be long now."

I heard two sets of footsteps walking away. "Don't leave me here," I called to them.

"Be a good girl, Alfhild." I heard the tell-tale clang of a heavy door swinging closed, and then footsteps walking over gravel.

They had gone.

I lay still for a minute, biding my time. And then another minute. And a third. The blood raced in my veins, and a beat throbbed in my forehead. I willed myself to remain calm. George wouldn't realise I had gone missing. I'd left him a note to tell him I'd be going back to the inn. My survival was down to me and me alone.

When I was sure the men weren't coming back, I twisted my hands in their bindings, envisioned the knots in my mind's eye. "*Solve fasciculos!*" I demanded and with relief felt the bindings slip against my skin as they gently loosened. I twisted my hands once more until I could free them from each other, then stiffly pushed myself into a sitting position and ripped the hood from my head. I stretched and loosened my fingers, groaning with the cramp in my arm. Hands shaking with effort and adrenaline, I unscrambled the knots of the rope around my feet.

Now I could stand and examine my surroundings. I found myself in a small barn or some farm outbuilding, bare of contents, apart from several piles of hessian sacks and large plastic bags that had been ripped open. They lay empty and discarded at the furthest end from me. I pushed a few around with my toe, but there was nothing there that would help me. Besides, an odd smell emanated from them. Something vaguely chemically. I assumed the bags had contained pesticides or something of use to the farm and dismissed them as useless.

The barn's walls were little more than rough planks of wood nailed to each other and cross beams. There were plenty of thin gaps, so I could peep between the slats. To my left, a sodium light lit up a row of tall and modern industrial units, all locked up for the night. To my right, I could spy a cottage or sturdy farm building about 200 feet away. Through the falling rain, I could see a few vehicles dotted around, and large puddles of water where the mud road had been churned up by heavy vehicles. There were lights on in the downstairs of the cottage and I imagined that this would be where my captors were hanging out.

I didn't have much time.

I tried the door but of course I'd heard the men lock it. In any case it was a sturdy iron door, in an iron surround with several locks on the outside. The walls were flimsier than the door. Perhaps I could break through a gap.

I quickly scanned the space again for something I could use as a tool, but the room was empty of anything that might prove useful. I spotted an iron cover in the floor though, with a rope handle, and quickly investigated. I yanked at the rope, and realised the door was heavier than it looked. I hauled with all my strength, finally making some headway and pulling it open by about 70 degrees. I peered into the opening, an inky vacuum. From what I could see, there was a drop to some kind of passage. In order to jump down into it, I'd have to fully open the door. I hauled with all my might to lift it until— once it had momentum—its own weight began to tip it backwards. At that stage, I couldn't hold on to it. It fell backwards with an impressive clang. The echo of that sounded impossibly loud in the relative stillness of the night.

With my heart in my mouth, I dashed back to the front wall of the barn and narrowed my eyes to stare through a tiny gap in the wall, my intestines squeezing in alarm. The cottage door opened, and someone stood on the front step, their face cast in shadow, but obviously staring my way.

I didn't have the luxury of any more time to think. I raced for the hole and dropped myself into it, tumbling down for about eight feet and landing with a painful thunk, knocking the air out of my lungs.

I spared myself ten seconds to try and allow my eyes to adjust. If it had been dark upstairs, the passage ahead was impossibly black, but I really had no choice now. Either I pressed on and trusted to fate or I had to stay and face who-knows-what.

I tentatively hauled myself to my feet. The passage—coarsely hewn from rock in places, and at other times carved out of the earth and fortified with roughly sawn timber—was barely wide enough for two people to pass and about eight feet high. I didn't like to think of the weight of earth and stone above me, in fact, I didn't want to think about anything at all. I simply had to get moving.

Without thinking twice, I began creeping along

the passage, my arms out, my fingers scraping against the walls. I took comfort in their solidity. Until now, I'd never really understood the shades of darkness that existed. The opening from above, with the faint chink from the external sodium lighting, lit my way for the first twenty metres or so, and my eyes gradually adjusted to the increasing blackness, allowing me to see further ahead for more time than I might have optimistically imagined. The problem was, my reluctance to rush headlong into the passage meant my captor had to have covered the two hundred feet to the barn in double-quick time and swiftly discovered my absence. I needed to press on more rapidly.

But I simply couldn't risk running into the pitch black. Instead, I warily held my hands out in front of me and trotted as hurriedly as my nerves would allow.

Water trickled down the stone walls, and I seemed to be heading along an incline. What if the only thing I found at the end of the passage was a pool of water? Or some sort of well? Perhaps this was all a trick? They had set a trap and I had walked into it. Rather than following me down here, they would simply close the door and leave me to a cold, miserable and lonely end.

Thinking in this way had me on the verge of hysteria.

Change your mind set, Alf, I scolded myself.

"What if none of that happens?" I demanded aloud. "What if I follow this passage all the way to Whittlecombe? What if I'm back at the inn in time for a hearty birthday breakfast? And everyone will gather round and sing Happy Birthday!"

I warmed to my theme. "George will be there! Gwyn and Charity, Dad and Florence and Zephaniah, Ned and Monsieur Emietter as well. And Millicent with Jasper and Sunny. Oh and Frau Kirsch! All the guests! And Luppitt and the Devonshire Fellows will regale me with their latest ballad. And it won't sound like strangled cats in an empty trunk. Mr Hoo will perch on the back of my chair and twit-twoo at me, and wobble his little head, and I'll scratch behind his ears. And I'll eat cake and dance. And I'll even be nice to Grandmama. For a day or two."

Tears pricked my eyes. "And I'll have made it to thirty-one in one piece!"

I wish you were all here with me.

"The loneliness of the long-distance passage," I said, trying to laugh, scraping my knuckles on the stone.

I'd stopped concentrating on where I was going. Big mistake. When the floor suddenly fell slightly away, I mis-stepped, jolting my knee painfully, falling forward with a grunt. I cast about me, checking for further traps or obstacles, then hauled myself back to standing. I reached out slowly with one foot, and taking it more carefully, my movements more tentative, my knee twinging, I found my way.

Three steps down and then the floor levelled out once more. I kept going, trying to calm my breathing as it rasped in and out of my throat. Many times I stopped to listen for noises behind me, and once or twice I even thought I heard something, steps behind me, or someone calling, but I turned my face forward and carried on. The isolation of my predicament ate away at my insides, and I yearned for the touch or the voice of another human being who cared about what happened to me.

I lost track of time and distance. I simply kept moving forwards, until finally I noticed I'd started an uphill climb. It seemed to me as though an hour had gone, maybe more, but the rate at which time passes, when you're walking through the pitch black in a long tunnel, can be deceptive I imagine. Nonetheless, my calves began to tire, and my lungs were working harder, and at last I imagined I had to be moving towards the surface.

My eyes ached with searching the darkness, and I realised that I might as well close them. I couldn't possibly see less. In fact, reaching out only with my senses—with one hand trailing against the wall, and the other out in front of me so I didn't fall flat on my face—proved to be the best way to move onwards. Unhindered by flights of fancy, or fears of what lurked in front of me, or who pursued me from behind, I concentrated only on moving forwards. I utilised my senses in the way that an owl or a bat might—throwing off invisible sonar and bouncing energy back at myself from the surfaces. Now, I started to make better progress.

I kept going, hoping that when I finally made it to the end of the passage, there would be no iron door barring my way, or no barrier preventing me freedom. To come all this way and still be trapped, well, that would be a serious miscalculation on my part.

The first hint I'd made it to the end came when a breath of cool air brushed across my cheek. Along with it came the scent of rain, replacing the stink of the cold mustiness of the passage. I opened my eyes, and yes, it might have been my imagination, but I felt the dark was a little less black. I walked more quickly, the climb steeper, my calf muscles working harder.

And then such relief!

Abruptly the small passage opened out into a cave, no bigger in size than The Snug back at Whittle Inn. I could clearly make out the wide opening ahead, through which I could see the rain falling. The darkness outside somehow managed to be so much more alive and vibrant than the pitch black of the tunnel behind me.

"Yes!"

The sound of jubilation erupted from me spontaneously and I made a dash for freedom, catapulting myself into the real world once more. I found myself three quarters of the way up a steep hill. The ground tumbled away from me to the forest below. Beyond the trees? I couldn't be sure, but twinkling lights in the distance might have been a town or a village, who knew?

That's where I intended to head next.

I took a step forward, experiencing a brief moment of recognition as I studied the landscape... something rang a bell in my head. But then before I could properly process what I was seeing, a low quiet voice came out of the darkness and I jumped out of my skin.

"Hello again, Alfhild." Innately calm but somehow distorted. Younger than the voice at the barn. Something familiar. "Happy birthday to you."

I didn't have time to look behind me, for even as I tried to, the stinking cloth had covered my face once more and I sank into oblivion.

"Hello again, Alfhild," he'd said. *"Hello again."*

I played the voice over and over in my fuddled mind. The intimacy of it. The calm self-assurance. It sounded so familiar. But I couldn't be totally sure. I wrestled with what I thought and what I knew. But I had no answers.

I lay in the dirt, hands and feet bound once more. They had gagged me this time, the rough material tied tightly, cutting into my mouth. The hood had been replaced, covering my head and knotted around my neck. But I wasn't back in the barn. They had brought me somewhere new, somewhere outside. The rain beat down on me, and my face pressed into the mud. The scent of damp vegetation, trees and grass, filled the air and I could almost taste the earth. But there was something more.

The sound of rain on water. Not running water. It was still, like a pool or a lake.

They had taken off my shoes and stockings, and my long robe. Clad only in my dress, the cold seeped off the soft ground beneath me, soaked into the thin material, and settled into my bones. I thought of the inn, and the huge fire in the bar. Oh to be wrapped in a blanket, snuggled on a chair in front of roaring flames.

I heard the familiar sound of tyres on a wet surface. A vehicle. We were close to a road. Listening intently, I could make out the occasional bark of a dog, and the scratching close by of small nocturnal animals, going about their business, unconcerned and undisturbed.

I wished with all my heart for Mr Hoo. He would be hunting. If only he could find me and bring help. If I could call him, would he hear? The gag in my mouth made it impossible for me to try.

Besides, I wasn't alone. They were both there, as far as I could tell, my pair of abductors. There may even have been more than two. But they worked in silence, not talking to each other and I could only sense their movements.

I thought they were constructing something. A heavy item. I heard one gasp as they hefted a substantial weight, and at some stage, the other said, "Careful!" and "Yes, that's it."

When they were done, one of them grabbed me by the upper arms and yanked me upright. The older chap, I discerned, with his voice closer to my ear. "Untie her feet," he ordered, obviously the one in charge. When I could walk, they pulled me a dozen or so steps forward.

"Okay," the older man said. While he continued to hold me firmly in his grasp, the younger one tied a rope around my middle.

"I know you're not religious, Alfhild. At least not in a biblical way. But did you know that in the Old Testament's book of Exodus, it says, 'Thou shalt not permit a sorceress to live'." He pulled on the rope around my middle. "Now while we do have a certain sympathy for you—after all, we're all cut from the same cloth, are we not? —we still have a job to do. There is no doubt of your guilt in the sorcery department. So regretfully I have taken it upon myself to act as judge and jury in this case and test whether you are truly guilty of witchcraft."

I wriggled, trying to break free of his grip, but when I moved I was encumbered by the rope, and something dragging me back. Bony fingers dug into my shoulder and I cried out, the sound muted by the gag.

"It has long been believed that water will reject the servants of the devil, and so I offer you to trial by water. Do you agree, Alfhild?"

I moaned into the gag. What foul deed were these two planning?

"Good, good." The older man's voice soothed. "I'll take that as acquiescence. Remember, if you are a witch and you float, then that is all the proof we need. We'll execute you as the sun comes up." His tone was light, confessional. I pulled harder to get away from him and the fingers dug so hard into my shoulder I was forced onto my knees.

"The good news is that you won't float, Alfhild. We've attached a bag of rocks to the rope around your middle."

I remembered the voice in the village hall the day in October when it had felt as though the whole village were against me; when the Gretchens, and Lyle had been stirring up so much trouble and bad feeling. There had been an anonymous speaker at the meeting. What was it he had said? *'In the old days we burned witches at the stake or drowned them in the village pond. Perhaps we should return to the old ways.'*

A red haze of panic tried to cloud my mind, but I pushed it fiercely away. Surely I would free myself using my innate abilities.

"Your magick will not help you here," sneered the older voice. As I tried one last time to wrench myself away from him, he lifted me as easily as a mother lifts her baby, and without much ado, threw me into the air.

The length of time between the launch and my hitting the water could only have been a second at the most, but time stretched interminably. The air rushed past me, and through the hood. Then the icy shock of freezing water snatched my breath away, and I was sinking, the hood working its way free as I sank to the bottom of the pool, my body dragged down by the weight of the bag of rocks, attached to my waist.

I twisted in the water, this way and that. Thrashing with my body, doubling over, making every effort to rip my hands from the rope that bound them. I tried and failed to utter the spell I'd used previously to untie my hands. Underwater I couldn't incant the words aloud. Desperately in need of air, I became increasingly weakened by my efforts.

I refused to resign myself to my fate. Eyes wide in the darkness, I stilled myself enough to send a plea out, to anyone, any being, magickal or otherwise, to find me. A single thought radiated from me – a pure message transmitted across the cosmos. *Help me.*

And so it was. Miracle of miracles, as my vision began to fade, I spotted a ghost light. Then two or three more. They darted forwards, curious, inquisitive, ready to help. They bobbed around me, waiting to be acknowledged.

"Come to me," I urged. With the last of my free will I watched as the lights became dark spectres. Three women with long hair streaming out behind them came into being, their clothes long and ragged, swirling in the water around them as they twirled and danced. They swam towards me, hands out in welcome, bathing me in their light.

CHAPTER THIRTEEN

"Hello? Hello?"

From a long distance a man's worried voice urgently called out, over and over again. Could they be talking to me? Couldn't they just let me sleep? I stretched stiffly, tried to open my eyes. Light. Too bright. I closed them again.

"Goodness me!" A woman. Familiar.

"Is she—?"

"No, she's moving." A soft hand pulled at my shoulder. "Hello? Hello, my love? Can you hear me?"

"Yes," I tried to say, but the words were stuck in my throat. Literally. I rolled back onto my front, coughed and retched, spitting up silt and pondweed and goodness knows what else. "Ugh," I groaned, and made an attempt to sit up, blinking into the light of a new day.

The rope was still around my hands but loosely tied. I tried to pull my hands free.

"What on earth?" The gentleman's voice exclaimed. "She's been tied up! I'm calling the police."

"I'm fine," I mumbled, expelling more water, blinking rapidly to clear my vision.

"You're hardly fine," said the tough, no-nonsense voice of my friend Millicent. I opened my eyes. Her dogs, Jasper and Sunny sniffed me in concern.

"Millicent?" I breathed. "Thank heavens it's you. Am I alive?"

"Of course you're alive, my lovely." She stared down at me, scanning my face, unsure of how I knew her. "Who did this to you?"

I pulled at her arm, bringing her closer to my mouth, "It's me, Alf."

"Alf?"

"Cosmetic alchemy," I explained, exhaustion washing through me, my teeth beginning to chatter with the cold.

Millicent turned to the gentleman standing behind her, keying a number into his phone. "She's fine," Millicent told him. "Could you call the local station and ask to be patched through to DS Gilchrist instead?" She glanced back at me.

"George has been out looking for you most of the night."

"He has?" I asked in confusion.

I pushed myself into a sitting position, a sudden wave of nausea rushing through me. The gentleman on the phone appeared to be speaking to George now.

"I want to go home," I lamented, feeling for all the world like a five-year-old in need of her mother.

"He's on his way. He won't be long," the gentleman told me, thumbing his phone off and then rapidly taking off his jacket to wrap around me.

"Th-th-thankyou," I shivered. "Sorry to put you to the trouble."

"It's no trouble at all," the old gent said. He sounded shocked and hurt on my behalf. "What happened?"

Millicent jumped in before I needed to respond. I was grateful to her, unable to think of a way to address his curiosity without him insisting on phoning someone besides George. "I think we should let DS Gilchrist ask all the questions," she said smoothly. "Don't you agree, Arthur?"

"I was at the Fayre," I said, as though that explained everything.

"Oh." The fellow nodded. "Yes, seems like

there's been lots of trouble there. Not sure they'll be granted another license again. Many of the villagers have been complaining about it. Some shady goings on, what with the fire, and people being ripped off, so I've heard."

"Yes." I shivered miserably. "I've heard the same."

"It's important not to tar everyone with the same brush," Millicent told the gentleman, and I let them go back and forth with their argument as I lapsed into miserable silence, my world grey around the edges. Millicent hugged me close and Jasper licked my face.

A car door slammed close by and looking up I watched as George raced towards us. "Alf," he cried. "Where have you been? What happened? I've been so worried!" He knelt in the mud beside me, taking one of my freezing hands in his warm ones. "You'll be the death of me, you will."

The world swayed on its axis. Ice lodged in my stomach at his words. "Don't say that," I gasped, hardly able to breathe. "Don't ever say that."

"It's alright," he soothed, but it wasn't. Fear gripped my intestines, twisting them painfully. If I'd had a vision played out on a movie screen, or Wizard Shadowmender's orb had shimmied into life and shown me the future, I couldn't have experienced this feeling of premonition more keenly.

I wrapped my arms around his neck. "Take me home," I begged. "I just want to be Alf again."

Do you remember how... when you were a kid and you contracted some horrible virus, everyone tip-toed around you while you slept in the semi-darkness? You were only half-aware of what was going on outside the safe haven of your own bed? That's how it was for me when I returned to Whittle Inn.

We arrived just before 6.30 am. The ghosts were preparing the inn for another day of our unique blend of hospitality, starting with breakfast of course. Monsieur Emietter and Florence were hard at it in the kitchen, frying sausages, grilling bacon and baking bread. Zephaniah was sweeping the bar and dining area. Ned was polishing glasses and setting the tables.

Charity had yet to make it downstairs, but as soon as she spotted George pulling up in the drive from her window, she hot-footed it downstairs to meet us.

"You've found her!" she cried. George helped me

to the door while Millicent steadied me from behind, the dogs sniffing anxiously around everyone. "What happened to you?" she asked taking my other arm. "Gwyn," she called up the stairs. "They've found her. She's back."

Gwyn appeared next to us, from nowhere, her face drawn with worry. "Alfhild!"

"I'm absolutely fine, Grandmama," I told her.

"Half drowned, soaked through and freezing cold, but absolutely fine," George said, his voice cross. "Quite clearly you aren't."

"What happened?" Charity asked. "Where have you been?"

I wanted to tell her, explain everything, but I was so cold and so tired, I couldn't even start. "Let me lie down," I begged. "And bring me a cup of tea, and then I'll tell you all."

"Of course," said Charity. "Let's get you upstairs."

I leaned heavily on my companions as they helped me to my room, listening to Grandmama barking orders at the other ghosts for toast and tea and extra blankets. I had thought to run a bath, or even simply jump in the shower, but as soon as I lay eyes on my bed, I could only hear the call of sleep - and that was it.

For the next few hours, I had a sense of people popping in and out. Someone soothing my forehead, George holding my hand, Gwyn repeatedly telling me everything was alright, and that I was home now. They wrapped me in love, and for a while I slept more peacefully.

I awoke, whimpering in fear, some time in the middle of the afternoon. Mr Hoo had taken a perch on the bedstead above my head. I swiped at tears as he hooted softly.

"I was dreaming," I told him.

"Hoo-ooo," he said, his eyes wise. "Hoo. Hooooo-ooo."

"I feel afraid," I said softly. "There's been a change in Whittlecombe and I'm worried that those I love will be hurt."

"Hooo." His tone seemed mournful. "Hoo?"

"Who indeed. I think we know, don't we?"

I threw back the covers. While I'd been sleeping, someone had added a couple of blankets to my quilt and now I was roasting. I stood, feeling a little shaky, noticing the grime embedded in my finger and toenails, the muck and grass stains covering my legs and arms. Thin arms. Bony wrists. I was still Fenella.

With renewed determination I marched into the bathroom and started running the bath. Usually I'd be reaching for the bubbles, but this time I extracted the Cosmetic Blaster Caster from where I'd hidden it in my underwear drawer, and then carefully removed it from its wrapping. Ostensibly it looked like a bath bomb, but it shimmered and vibrated in my hand, coloured vaguely pink. I tossed it into the hot water and watched it as it erupted—an extravagant soap bomb—spinning around the bath, effervescing, popping and fizzing, alive with vital and purposeful energy.

I ran the water as hot as I could physically stand. When the bath was almost full, I gingerly stepped in, gasping at the temperature of the water, and easing my aching bones down. I stared at all the contusions and bruises. The marks on my wrists and ankles where the rope had chafed, red and sore.

But cuts and bruises heal. Time sees to that.

Whereas nothing would take away the experience of what I'd been through. Those emotions would remain raw for now.

I fully intended to put it all behind me, the abduction, the horror of making my way through the impossibly dark passage, the nightmare of being half-drowned. Someone had tried to use the old penalty of swimming a witch in the village pond on me. The terror of that would live with me for a long time.

And I would never forget. What doesn't kill you makes you stronger.

Fenella had served her purpose. Now it was time for me to be Alf again.

I slipped down under the water, submerging my head, and as I did so, the memory of the previous evening flashed back to me, in technicolour brilliance.

Even in the heat of the bath, I could remember the frigid temperature of the village pond, and how surprisingly deep it had been. The bag of rocks, tied to the rope around my middle had quickly fallen towards the bottom, dragging me down with more speed than I ever could have guessed. The water had pressed in on me. The darkness complete. Despite fighting to free my hands, chafing the skin at my wrists badly, I'd made little progress. No progress.

It had been overwhelming. Suffocating.

But those lights... ghost lights...

In the final moments of rational consciousness, I'd recognised the glow. Understood them to be what they were, the lights of souls lost in the water. And by acknowledging them, I'd facilitated their appearance, these unfortunate women, once ducked in the pond by suspicious witch finders.

I'd never known that witches had been subject to persecution in Whittlecombe centuries before. Yet how could I have dared to imagine that the subjugation of my kind had passed this tiny village by?

There may well have been a Daemonne woman or two among them.

Once I'd called the ghost lights to me, they'd manifested into their mortal physique, while maintaining an element of their spiritual guise. They were at once human-shaped and yet simultaneously transparent, with a supernatural glow. They lit up the world under the surface of the pond, darting around me, shimmering trails following in their wake. Bubbles erupting from them as they displaced the water, and each tiny air ball shone like a miniscule aquatic glow worm.

The women moved around me, their heads cocked with curiosity, their eyes burning with life that had yet to be extinguished. With hair streaming about them, fanning out like strands of pondweed, they reached for me, their flesh the colour of a fish's underbelly. When I breathed the water in, unable to hold my breath any longer, they wrapped me in a nurturing embrace and swam through the water with me.

I could remember the colours, the flash of a thousand shades of green and yellow and gold and brown. I remember studying the pebble lined silt of the bottom of the pond in excruciating detail, the shape of every piece of grit indelibly burned on my mind. Rusting bicycles and broken toys littered the floor. And coins-aplenty—thrown for luck. I probed the broken crockery and the bony remains of a once-cherished cat with curiosity, and swam around pointing out buttons, bricks, and one of a pair of roller skates.

I could no longer feel the cold. I danced with the women, my dress whirling around me, limbs free, unencumbered. At some stage when the rain stopped in the world above us, we swam close to the surface. I studied the waning moon—surrounded by twinkling stars—through the lens of the water. The clouds floated across the sky so high above us, on a completely different plane to the one I temporarily inhabited.

I knew I couldn't stay. The women guided me back to land when the coast was clear. How I made it from the water to the bank I have no idea. The next thing I remembered was the shocked voice of old

Arthur, and Millicent out for an early morning walk with her dogs.

Now, completely submerged in my bath, holding my breath and waiting to live as Alf again, I recalled those women with their pale, pale skin and deep black eyes, and I sent them love and gratitude.

Beneath the surface of the village pond, lay a world of forgotten and ancient magick.

Perhaps that forgotten and ancient magick was at the heart of everything that was happening in Whittlecombe? I didn't know.

When my lungs could hold out no longer, I burst through the water with a loud gasp. Cascades of red hair clung to my shoulders. Thicker thighs and a rounder belly than Fenella's poked from the water. I wiggled my little toes—so crooked and ugly—and felt a rush of warmth as I took in the reassuring smattering of freckles on the backs of my hands.

My own beautiful flaws. No-one else's.

Mr Hoo settled on the window and chirruped happily. He seemed content.

The Cosmetic Blaster Caster had performed its miracle.

I grinned with relief and relaxed into the water once more.

Alf was home.

Florence popped into my room with fresh towels as I was drying my hair.

Or at least that's how she wanted it to appear.

She loitered by my bed as I attacked my wild mop with a comb. Never had I been so glad to have such a rich tangle of untameable curls. I was in no hurry to sport a sleek black bob again.

"Are you alright, Florence?" I asked.

She nodded, folding her bundle of towels for about the eight time. "What is it?" I asked.

She looked around, checking for mortals and spirits. "Miss Alf," she whispered. "I did as you asked and checked on Mr Wylie a few times."

Mr Wylie? I'd forgotten about him. The unexpected guest.

"And?"

She shrugged. "He checked out this morning after you were brought home."

I nodded. *What a coincidence.* "Did he give a reason? Say he was going home or moving on or anything?"

"No, just thanked us for our hospitality."

That seemed normal enough. He had been a man of few words, that much was obvious.

But Florence hadn't finished. "While he was here, I... investigated... his room. He had a couple of suits in the wardrobe, and half a dozen white shirts and ties, and very little else. He went out every day, to meet clients. He would come back and have a drink at the bar and chat with Zephaniah and Charity most nights. He had very plain tastes in food – he ordered plain omelette for breakfast and meat and potatoes for dinner. No vegetables, no sauces. Monsieur Emietter was most put out."

"Oh, okay." That all sounded straight-forward enough though. Why had I been worried?

And why did Florence look so perturbed?

"So... what's the problem then?"

"When he was in the bar one evening I went up to his room to look in his briefcase." Florence looked troubled, her singed brows knot closely together on her sooty face.

"And?" This was getting interesting.

"*And*... there was nothing whatsoever in it."

I stopped combing my hair. My hand poised in mid-air. Now it was my turn to look perplexed. "Nothing? What do you mean nothing?"

"It was completely empty. Not even a paperclip."

"How come you were looking for me?" I quizzed George later. We were seated round the kitchen table with Millicent and Charity. Monsieur Emietter carried on chopping vegetables and making soup, while Florence hovered close by, half an eye on the French chef, and half an eye on my plate and mug, intent on making me feel better by feeding me up.

The kitchen was warm. I had donned my thickest pyjamas and dressing gown but still the feeling of ice in my marrow pervaded. I wrapped my hands around my mug and hunched down into my collar, until Gwyn appeared with a soft wool shawl and draped it over my shoulders.

"I'd taken shelter in The Hay Loft while it rained. The weather was so awful, wasn't it? I figured I'd join you in the caravan later. When I walked back to the camping field past the booth I could see you'd gone, but when I arrived at the caravan you weren't there. I found the note you'd written crumpled up under the steps."

"I was going to leave it on your sleeping bag where you'd see it."

George nodded. "I thought it odd that you'd crumpled the note up, and when I looked under the caravan I found your rucksack with the orb in it. I knew you wouldn't have stowed it under there. Especially not in that weather."

"They must have kicked it under there." I shivered at the memory of how they'd ambushed me. All that, less than twenty-four hours before. "It's lucky they never thought to look for the orb."

"So where did they take you?" Charity asked.

I thought about it. "I'm honestly not sure." George looked disappointed at my words. "I was completely out of it when they put me in the car or van or whatever, so I don't know how long we were driving."

"Car or van?" George had his notebook out and his pen poised.

I considered this. "Van."

"Sure?"

"Absolutely. It was uncomfortable. I wasn't on a seat. No upholstery. I was lying on the flat bed of the back of a van. And when we went around the beds, my back was supported by a wall."

"And the engine?"

"Deep. Clunky. A diesel. But not a big truck, so maybe the size of a parcel van or something. Like the post office use."

George wrote that down. "What did you see when you arrived?"

"Nothing. I had a hood on. I couldn't see anything at first. They left me there. Tied up. I heard a big heavy iron door. I used an untangling spell to free my hands and that allowed me to rip the hood off." I thought back to those moments. I'd managed to quell my terror, positive that one way or another I would get out of that situation. "I was being kept in a barn, a small barn, or an outbuilding."

"On a farm?" George asked.

I recalled the muddy track between the barn and the cottage. Remembered the smell of manure. "A dairy farm. I could smell cows!"

"Great!" George exclaimed. "Now we're getting somewhere."

Charity smiled and squeezed my arm. "You're doing brilliantly. You were so brave."

I patted her hand. "I had to come back. I wanted to be with you guys again."

"Can you remember anything else?" George remained all business-like.

"The tunnel I told you about. It felt like a long tunnel. Underground. Dug out beneath the earth. It opened into a smallish cave, and when I exited the cave I could see lights in the distance. I didn't really have time to work out whether it was Whittlecombe or where I was."

"How many lights?"

I shook my head. That part was a blur. "Not many I think."

"Any moving lights? Could you tell if there was a main road somewhere?"

"I don't think so. They were pretty static ..." I racked my brain. What had I seen? A red light. On the top of something tall. Not tall enough to be a mobile phone mast. But—

"The big wheel."

"You saw the big wheel from the Fayre?" Charity repeated.

I nodded, emphatic now. "Yes. That means the hill overlooked Whittlecombe, doesn't it?"

George nodded happily. "That's a good start. I can check out all the farms within a three-mile radius for starters. There'll be plenty with lock ups and outbuildings, so it might not narrow it down a great deal, but not all of them will be dairy farms. Just getting eyes-on will be useful at this stage."

"Piddlecombe Farm," I said hesitantly.

"What about it? Was that the name of where you were?" George's pen was poised to write that down.

"Rob mentioned it. It has lock-ups that they rent out. He keeps his catering vans there."

"I know Piddlecombe. It had been in the same family for years," Charity said. "But it changed hands a few years ago."

"All above board, do you reckon?" George asked her.

"Well now that you come to mention it, I don't know. The old fella that used to live there just disappeared. I think everyone assumed he'd passed on and sold up." Charity thought for a second. "I don't know the new owners."

George closed his notebook with a snap. "I think I'll check that one first, while we still have some light."

Ice crystallised in my insides once more. "Do you have to go out now?"

"Make hay while the sun shines, isn't that what they say?"

"It will still be shining tomorrow," I protested.

Charity joined in. "That's true, George," and she narrowed her eyes and nodded at Florence. George glanced from Charity to me and then at Florence, who quickly disappeared into the pantry.

"Oh yes," he said.

Charity was as subtle as a sledgehammer.

A beaming Florence returned to the kitchen, a large birthday cake floating through the air ahead of her. I couldn't see what flavour it was, but it had been covered in pale green icing, with pretty jasmine-type flowers as decoration, and a miniature wonky inn, and an owl—both modelled in edible clay —alongside a witch's hat on the top.

"Happy birthday to you," sang Charity, completely tunelessly, and the others joined in.

Talk about a cats' chorus. I smiled, grimaced and laughed at the same time.

"Blow out the candles! Blow out the candles!" Charity called excitedly, and I leaned forward to extinguish thirty-one tiny glowing torches with one big breath.

Florence clapped her hands. "Now you can make a wish."

I closed my eyes tight and wished for my heart's desire, and when I opened them again, I gazed around at the people I loved the most—with only my father Erik missing—with grim eyes. *Keep them safe,* I'd wished.

Help me to keep them safe.

Forty minutes later, I was full of freshly baked cake, hot tea, and good cheer. I'd unwrapped presents from Charity (a book about meditation) and Gwyn (the collected works of P G Wodehouse) and now I was standing on the front step of Whittle Inn to see George off as he headed to Piddlecombe Farm on what was probably a wild goose chase.

He hugged me close, and I inhaled his signature scent. Something fresh and lemony in either his aftershave or washing powder, and the warm musk of a busy detective.

"A couple of pieces of good news," he said.

"Mm?" I breathed him in.

"Rob is home from the hospital and recuperating. And I heard that Mr Bramble is responding well to treatment in the hospital after his heart attack."

"Oh, that is good news." I was pleased to hear that.

"He'll need looking after for a while. Like you."

"I'll be fine."

I felt his smile against my cheek. "I left your birthday present on your bed."

"You've been in my room?" I asked in mock horror. "What will Grandmama say?"

He chuckled, and I felt the laugh vibrate through his chest. "It was she who put it there for me."

"Ah, did she? Fair enough." We pulled apart. "You pair of collaborators."

"I'd take you out this evening if you were up to it."

I shook my head. I knew he would. "I'm really not. I feel as rough as old boots. I'll have an early night and we can regroup in the morning. Maybe go out tomorrow night?"

"The Hay Loft?" He raised his eyebrows with all innocence.

"You can bog off," I retorted.

This time his laugh came from his belly. He kissed me and headed for his car, waving as he slipped behind the wheel, then beeping his horn as he ambled down the drive.

I waved even when he was out of sight, as though he would feel me wishing him well and sending my love. I felt alone without his arms around me. The icy sensation in my stomach seemed to be taking up permanent residence.

Yet today, I should be celebrating.

I was thirty-one. I'd made it, despite the death threats. The Mori had failed in their mission to finish me off.

However, as I watched George's tail lights disappear down the lane, I couldn't help feeling they weren't done with me yet.

An hour later, I excused myself from Charity and Gwyn and climbed back up the stairs to my rooms, carrying Grandmama's choice of reading material and Charity's meditation manual. My hair had dried as much as it was going to after my bath, and now I tied it up in a messy bun and slipped off my dressing gown. The sun wouldn't set for another hour or so, but I intended to have a little me time and recoup some of my spent energy.

I found George's neatly wrapped parcel on my pillow, a small package wrapped in white tissue paper and tied with pink ribbon. I could only assume he'd had it wrapped in store. I couldn't imagine George being able to tie anything with such an intricate bow.

I tugged at the ribbon and dropped it onto the bed, then slit the tissue paper with my nail, loath to rip the paper. Inside I found a navy-blue jewellery box, and so I pulled open the lid, expecting a pair of earrings or something similar.

I gasped.

A slip of paper tumbled out, revealing a black onyx stone, flanked by two diamonds, all set together on a slim white-gold band.

I plucked the slip of paper from my lap where I'd caught it.

My darling Alf

Perhaps this is a promise of good times together?

If you'd do me the honour?

Yours, with love everlasting

George G X

PS. I thought you'd prefer black.

"Oh my," I stuttered, resisting the urge to cry and laugh at the same time.

I heard tittering from beyond the door. I rolled my eyes, hopped off the bed and walked over to fling it open. Charity, Florence and Gwyn stood outside, eyes wide with anticipation.

We regarded each other in seriousness for a moment, then when I could resist no longer, I shrieked and jumped up and down and they rushed in and mobbed me.

"Are you going to say yes?" Charity demanded, as she wrapped me in a bear hug, Gwyn and Florence creating a draft as they flitted around us.

"Well, I don't know," I said, secretly as pleased as punch—although I'm sure that was obvious—as I showed off the ring, waving my hand around at everyone. "It's all a bit sudden. He said we could go out tomorrow night so maybe we can discuss it properly then."

"He needs to get down on one knee and propose properly, Miss Alf," Florence insisted.

"Oh fiddle-faddle," I said, but part of me figured she was right. Perhaps I'd see to it.

At that moment the phone on my night table began to ring. I picked it up. George.

I beamed at the others and waved them out if the room as I accepted the call. "Out, out!" I told them, and they scurried away giggling as I closed the door after them to give myself some privacy.

"Hello," I said into the phone, trying to play it cool as my heart fluttered in my chest.

"Alf," a breathy gasp.

I stopped everything, senses on high alert. That freezing sensation in my guts spread throughout my body.

"George?"

"Listen to me carefully, I haven't got long."

"George—" Panic rose like bile in my throat.

He cut me off. "Alf. Remember what we found in Derek Pearce's shed? The white crystals? I think more of that has been stored here. Those bags you say you saw when you were held in the barn? I've found them. They're labelled as dangerous chemicals."

"You're at Piddlecombe Farm?" I asked.

"Yes. I'm absolutely certain this is where you were held last night. From what you described."

"Okay," I said, keeping it together as best as I was able. "So get out of there."

"I can't Alf. They're here."

"Who is there?" I asked desperately.

"The Mori." He breathed softly. "There's dozens of them here."

What did he mean. "Spinning globes?"

"Yes."

This couldn't be happening. No wonder I'd had such a bad feeling all day. "Get out of there, George," I begged. "Just run. Go back to your car. Drive fast. Please come home."

I heard an odd whirring noise from his end of the phone. He was silent for too long.

"George?" I cried down the line.

I heard him groan. The whirring louder than ever. "I love you, Alfie. Stay safe."

The line went dead.

EPILOGUE

I made two calls.

The first to Wizard Shadowmender via the orb. I told him everything. About my night of horror, the women in the pond, about George, about the chemicals he'd found, and about the mysterious Mr Wylie. I placed him—and through him—all of our kind on high alert

The second to the police. They needed to know that one of their own was missing.

I sat by my phone, waiting for news, twisting the ring on my left finger with my right hand. My stomach churned with anxiety. The rope burns bright against my pale skin.

One of George's colleagues called me the following evening. They had searched Piddlecombe Farm and found nothing of note. George's car had been found—torched—in a local beauty spot in a cliff top car-park in Durscombe.

There was no evidence that George had been in the car when it had been set on fire.

The police were launching a search and rescue mission along the coast.

I knew they wouldn't find him.

Dark clouds were gathering over Whittlecombe and The Mori were biding their time.

Some time soon they would show their hand, and when they did, I'd be waiting for them.

My heart broken, I settled back to play the waiting game.

ACKNOWLEDGEMENTS

Huge thanks as always to my sensational street team, and a shout-out to my ARC readers over on Booksprout who have been so effusive and supportive as regards the Wonky Inn Books. I have been completely taken aback by the love I've had for Alf and her friends.

Special thanks to JC Clarke of The Graphics Shed for her phenomenal covers, and to Anna Bloom once more, for her sensible suggestions and common-sense approach, her passion and her belief.

To my husband John for his love and support, and my friends, real and virtual, who cheer me on when the going gets tough.

Finally, most importantly, thanks to you, the reader. I

love bringing you my stories, reading your reviews, and receiving your feedback. You complete my circle.

Much love ♥

Jeannie Wycherley
Devon, UK
31st January 2019

WONKY CONTINUES

The Mystery of the Marsh Malaise:
Wonky Inn Book 5

Water, water everywhere ... but not a drop to drink. Alfhild Daemonne's beloved Speckled Wood is dying. When several Whittlecombe locals are taken seriously ill, she discovers that the water in and around the village has been poisoned.

The wonky inn owner knows full well her bitter arch-rivals The Mori are out to do serious harm to her reputation, her business, and the land she cherishes - and yet she's the one being scapegoated. Once again, the villagers have placed the blame firmly at poor Alf's door.

Meanwhile, the ancient and magickal Keeper of the Marsh, an ancient tree named Vance, is furious with her.

She's going to have to mollify him.

And that won't be easy.

Is Alf up to fighting The Mori alone? Can she gather the right experts who will help her in the battle to clear her name?

And will she be able to appease Vance and therefore cleanse the springs and marshes around the village?

Find out in this action-packed instalment of the wonky inn series, full to bursting with the ghosts, witches, wizards, warlocks and weirdness you've come to adore. Clean and cozy with subtle hints of darkness.

Available on Amazon

ADD SOME MAGICKAL SPARKLE

Christmas at Wonky Inn

Add some magickal sparkle to your Christmas with a Christmas Wonky Novella

The Witch Who Killed Christmas

It's an ill wind that blows no good...
An unexpected snowmageddon threatens to derail Christmas at Alfhild Daemonne's inn.

She's hosting her first festive celebration, so she's understandably disappointed when guests begin cancelling bookings, thanks to the abnormal wintery conditions in the south west of England.

When Alf receives information that there may be an ulterior reason for the weather anomaly, she journeys deep into the forest in search of a witch with an attitude problem.

Can Alf save Christmas at Wonky Inn? Or will one mean old witch kill Christmas for everyone?

The Witch Who Killed Christmas can be read as a standalone or as part of the Wonky Inn series.

THE BIRTH OF WONKY

In Case You Missed the Birth of Wonky

The story begins...

The Wonkiest Witch: Wonky Inn Book 1

Alfhild Daemonne has inherited an inn.
and a dead body.

Estranged from her witch mother, and having
committed to little in her thirty years, Alf surprises
herself when she decides to start a new life.

She heads deep into the English countryside intent
on making a success of the once popular inn.
However, discovering the murder throws her a curve
ball. Especially when she suspects dark magick.

Additionally, a less than warm welcome from several locals, persuades her that a variety of folk – of both the mortal and magickal persuasions – have it in for her.

The dilapidated inn presents a huge challenge for Alf. Uncertain who to trust, she considers calling time on the venture.

Should she pack her bags and head back to London? Don't be daft.

Alf's magickal powers may be as wonky as the inn, but she's dead set on finding the murderer.

Once a witch always a witch, and this one is fighting back.
A clean and cozy witch mystery.

Take the opportunity to immerse yourself in this fantastic new witch mystery series, from the author of the award-winning novel, Crone.

Grab Book 1 of the Wonky Inn series, The Wonkiest Witch, right here

PLEASE?

If you have enjoyed reading *Fearful Fortunes and Terrible Tarot*, please consider leaving me a review.

Reviews help to spread the word about my writing, which takes me a step closer to my dream of writing full time.

If you are kind enough to leave a review, please also consider joining my Author Street Team on Facebook – Jeannie Wycherley's Fiendish Street Team. Do let me know you left a review when you apply because it's a closed group. You can find my fiendish team at https://www.facebook.com/groups/JeannieWycherleysFiends/

You'll have the chance to Beta read and get your hands on advanced review eBook copies from time to time. I also appreciate your input when I need some help with covers, blurbs etc.

Or sign up for my newsletter http://eepurl.com/cN3Q6L to keep up to date with what I'm doing next!

The Wonky Inn Series

ALSO BY

Beyond the Veil (2018)

Crone (2017)

A Concerto for the Dead and Dying (short story, 2018)

Deadly Encounters: A collection of short stories (2017)

Keepers of the Flame: A love story (Novella, 2018)

Non Fiction

Losing my best Friend Thoughtful support for those
affected by dog bereavement or pet loss (2017)

Follow Jeannie Wycherley

Find out more at on the website
www.jeanniewycherley.co.uk

You can tweet Jeannie twitter.com/Thecushionlady

Or visit her on Facebook for her fiction

www.facebook.com/jeanniewycherley

Sign up for Jeannie's newsletter
http://eepurl.com/cN3Q6L

Coming Soon

Coming Spring 2019

The Municipality of Lost Souls by Jeannie Wycherley

Described as a cross between Daphne Du Maurier's *Jamaica Inn*, and TV's *The Walking Dead*, but with ghosts instead of zombies, *The Municipality of Lost Souls* tells the story of Amelia Fliss and her cousin Agatha Wick.

In the otherwise quiet municipality of Durscombe, the inhabitants of the small seaside town harbour a deadly secret.

Amelia Fliss, wife of a wealthy merchant, is the lone voice who speaks out against the deadly practice of the wrecking and plundering of ships on the rocks in Lyme bay, but no-one appears to be listening to her.

As evil and malcontent spread like cholera

throughout the community, and the locals point fingers and vow to take vengeance against outsiders, the dead take it upon themselves to end a barbaric tradition the living seem to lack the will to stop.

Set in Devon in the UK during the 1860s, *The Municipality of Lost Souls* is a Victorian Gothic ghost story, with characters who will leave their mark on you forever.

If you enjoyed *Beyond the Veil*, you really don't want to miss this novel.

Sign up for my newsletter or join my Facebook group today.

Made in the USA
Middletown, DE
09 August 2020